His Second Chance

An Enemies to Lovers Romance

Love Comes to Town Book 4

ASHLEE PRICE

https://www.ashleepriceromanceauthor.com/

CHAPTER 1

Wynona

He wouldn't dare.

But the longer I sit on my cushioned wicker seat, the harder it is to deny it.

I grip the monogrammed S&N cupcake I'm holding hard.

Whoever's wearing five times skunkier perfume than need be, I want to punch them. Almost as much as I want to punch him.

That's our song, all right.

He doesn't say the words, but he doesn't need to. As his hands glide over the piano keys, I can hear them in my head.

Past, present, future, you are

Whenever I'm far away

It's time to say

I gotta get back to you

I gotta get back to you...

"Liar," I hiss under my breath.

And the way he's looking at me with that beautifully sculpted face with its tousled blond hair and blue eyes I already know all too well can be about fifteen different shades depending on his mood...

Emerson Fucking Storm.

The whole reason I shouldn't have come.

But then again, Sierra Hill—no, now Sierra Storm—is my best friend. I couldn't abandon her at her wedding, of all times.

Now, get this, the song's over and done with and Emerson is the one walking off, looking thoughtful and sad.

As if he were the one who'd had the past cruelly dredged up.

He tries looking my way, but I'm prepared. I've had twenty-six years to perfect this glare of mine.

If glares could kill, mine would've made Emerson explode in a nice puff of red and black confetti so a nice old janitor who looks like Bill Nye could sweep him up.

Alas, no such luck.

"Uh, Winnie?" Josie whispers, elbowing me.

"What?" I snap.

Her sparkly pale face, with its powdery blue sparkly eye shadow and, you guessed it, sparkly pink gloss, has a holier-than-thou expression I'm so not in the mood for. "If you really hate the cupcakes, you could, you know, just not take one?"

I glare at her until I realize that she has a point.

That makes two cupcakes I've smooshed to an untimely death on my gold-rimmed plate.

Whoops.

"Maybe we should get drunker?" Josie suggests with a quirked strawberry-blonde eyebrow, her eyes already on the bar.

I quirk my own black-lined eyebrow back at her. "Were you not there when Sierra gave her very kind, very firm talk about when to get shit-faced and when not to?"

"The wedding's over with," she points out. "They're about to start the music now that Emerson has played a few pieces. I'd say now is as good a time as any."

I make a skeptical noise.

"Suit yourself," Josie says, bobbing upright with more energy than I've had since I was about four years old. "I, for one, am going to enjoy tonight."

I wave at her. "Have fun."

Josie pauses, guilt finding its way onto her cheerful face as she leans in. "I'm sorry, Wyn. I know this is hard. Maybe if you just—"

"No," I say sharply, shaking my head for emphasis. "We already discussed this."

Josie says loudly, "I know. But if you just told Sierra—"

"Told me what?" Sierra says, her gorgeous shimmering pouf of a wedding gown billowing around her as she approaches our table.

"Nothing," Josie and I trill at the same time.

Sierra just laughs, although her gaze softens when it stops on me. "Honestly, Wyn, if you have to go off and cry or need me to be there for you, I can be. Even if it's my wedding day, you just went through the breakup of all breakups."

Halfway through her speech, I'm already shaking my head. "No can do, Sierra. I am a selfish bitch, but not that much of a selfish bitch."

"Honestly," she says, smile broadening as she sneaks a look back at her new husband, Nolan, "nothing could ruin today for me. And after you made that... sacrifice as far as the bridesmaid's dress is concerned..."

I aim a glare at Josie, the one who chose it, who's smiling innocently. "Don't worry, I don't blame you for the..." monstrosity, mockery, punishment "color."

Just then, the first song of the night booms on. Oh, listen up, here's a story about a little guy that lives in a blue world...

Sierra throws her perfectly done reddish-brown hair back and cackles as she looks at me. "That song, Blue? You didn't!"

"I did," I say, smiling despite myself as I rise. "I had to get some good stuff on that playlist with all the Michael Bublé, Backstreet Boys, and Spice Girls Josie insisted on slipping in there."

"I've heard you singing Stop Right Now in the shower," Josie accuses me blandly, rising too.

I just shrug, although she has a point. "There's no telling what drunk me will do."

And that's the problem, isn't it?

The reason I can't drink away my sorrows, as per usual.

Because there is a big mistake here I have no plans to repeat.

And his name is Emerson Storm.

But as Sierra, Josie, and I get to the dance floor and groove our hearts out and I grab one more drink—just one—I almost forget.

I'm almost back there, sixteen years old, at the first rave I snuck into with them. We all had matching pink synthetic wigs and white velvet American Apparel dresses, and we spent most of the night exploring the abandoned factory the rave was in when we weren't giggling at any guy who tried to talk to us or dancing so hard we were out of breath. We'd requested this song from the DJ so many times he'd ended up flipping us off.

We were still immature, stupid kids then. Things were still easy in the way they are before you grow up.

When the song's done, I'm already dead tired. Might be thanks to the part when we all started jumping frantically. Or where Josie and I lifted Sierra to our shoulders, the three of us laughing and laughing.

Or maybe it's how, near the end of the song, I saw him.

He stood off to the side, looking at me as if I were some kind of physical barrier between him and the dance floor. As if I were the one who'd ruined things all those years ago.

"I'm going to take a breather," I tell my friends, even though we're already outside and it's already cool.

But a breather for me means—has always meant—being alone. Quiet. Having space to think.

Even though that last part rarely does me much good.

It takes me a few minutes of walking down the beach, away from the music and the happy wedding party and away from the odd hotel beach lounger and romantic couple, before I'm really alone. Finally.

I plunk my butt in the sand and stare out into the roiling waves. Advance, advance, advance... crash.

Closer, closer, closer... crash.

A lone gull from somewhere wheels. Somewhere further off, someone whoops.

I don't know why, but I've never felt lonelier than when I hear other people having fun when I'm not.

I close my eyes and inhale deeply.

I can smell the salt in the air, taste it.

I let my heeled feet dig into the sand, let my head fall back.

Ah, now this—this was exactly what I needed.

Suddenly, my back stiffens.

My eyes are closed, and there hasn't been so much as a sound or murmur out of place, yet... I know.

Someone's here.

"Imagine seeing you here," an all-too-familiar voice says.

CHAPTER 2

Emerson

Goddamn, does she look good.

Same thin body, even fitter now. You can see it in those colorful tatted-up arms.

Yes, that's Wynona Cowell, all right.

Same pale triangle of a face. Same hair the color of ravens. Same lip piercing and bright red lipstick I want to taste.

I wonder, does she still kiss the same?

Her cold voice breaks my reverie. "What do you want?"

"Just to talk," I say, sitting down beside her.

She keeps staring out at the waves. She always had a way of doing that, zoning out when things got tough. Not that I was much better.

"I don't have anything to say to you," she says, her voice firm.

"Listen," I say. "I'm sorry about before, but—"

Next thing I know, she's on her feet, glaring at me again. That same glare that now wants me to throw myself into the ocean and not come out.

"Don't do this," she hisses, stalking off.

I can't stop myself. I follow. "Won't you give me a chance to explain?"

She throws herself forward as fast as those toned legs can carry her. "What's there to explain, Emerson? There is no reasonable reason for you to have played that song. Yet you did."

"I didn't mean to," I growl. "I was just lost in thought, and… it just happened. It felt good. Like seeing an old friend again. I hadn't played it for a long time, not since—"

"Don't." She freezes, stabbing out a finger at me. "Just don't, okay? These past few days have been hard enough already. Didn't you notice how I was avoiding you?"

"Yeah, I noticed," is all I can think to say.

She keeps walking. So do I.

"Tonight is about Sierra," she says firmly. "I'm not going to make some scene and then have to explain to her why I never mentioned that you were my ex. The ex."

"The ex," I repeat with a little chuckle. "Guess I should be flattered?"

She stops dead and gives me another one of those signature glares of hers. "No. You shouldn't be. Believe me."

As she continues away, head held high, I call after her, "No temporary truce, even?"

She lets the blossom-scented breeze carry my question away.

I stand there, feet rooted in the sand, like a complete idiot.

I guess I deserve this. What the hell else did I think would happen?

Hell, it's been over five years now, and the last time Wynona and I spoke…

I grind my teeth.

No. It's better not to think of that.

Better to just drink and drink some more—not enough to worry my older brothers, though. They're still a bit overprotective after that incident some months back, as much as they profess to admire me for 'how far I've come'.

Just a drink or two. I've only had one so far, after all.

Just to dull the edge.

Nostalgia's a bitch, and I haven't been able to cut out that particular bad habit of looking back. Not yet, at least.

Heading back to the wedding reception tents on the beach is calming.

Jeremy gives me a wave, headed the opposite direction. Guess I'm lucky Nolan let me invite my childhood friend along, especially when he's never been crazy about the guy. But I did have an unused plus-one, so...

Anyway, I ditched my shoes on the way here, so I get to feel the massage of the damp sand between my toes.

The murmur and rhythmic whish of the waves gets my breathing slower and on board too.

I've always meant to compose a song to the sound.

I've made songs for lots of things—birthdays, trees, a certain ex I encountered tonight who I'm better off not thinking about... but not waves. Not yet.

There are so many things I'd still like to do. So many things I wish I hadn't.

I'm not a good man. Not half the man I should be.

My phone goes off.

I check it with excitement, then scowl, rejecting the call.

That is just about the last thing I need right now.

"There you are!" Nolan says as I approach the pavilion, jogging over to me, his long dark hair swaying behind him. "I was beginning to worry that you'd taken a midnight swim and ditched us."

"I was nine when I did that," I remind him, although I'm smiling despite myself. "And don't you have a beautiful bride to woo?"

Nolan groans. "Knew there was something I was forgetting…"

We crack up, and he throws his arm around me. "Seriously, though, we've danced together for every other song. Now, there's someone I'd like for you to meet."

I know that tone all too well. "I appreciate it, Nolan, but I'm not in the mood for—"

"Too late," he says mischievously, grabbing a paunchy, sunburnt man. "Emerson, meet Yolan. Yolan, meet my brother. AKA the one who was playing the piano."

As Nolan glides away, sneaky as an eel, the paunchy man's patchy face lights up. "Ah. So, it was you on that piano up there? Jesus, you were good! I didn't see who it was, accidentally got some aloe vera cream in my eye while I was trying to soothe my face." He giggles. "Anyway, how would you like to go on tour sometime? I have a group of classical musicians who tour, and…"

I play along with the man as we chat for the next few minutes. He probably means well. They all do.

Thing is, you can't take a man too seriously when he's three drinks in. And I've had too many amazing drunken plans—for a South American road trip, an impromptu hike to Boston, a duet with a celebrity, a concert to raise money for poor orphans in Chile—fall through in the weeks afterward to take anything planned over too many drinks very seriously. Even if a tour would be really awesome.

While my career as a pianist hasn't exactly stalled, it hasn't really been taking off lately either.

And to think of everything I gave up…

My hand tightens on the deep red cocktail I didn't even notice getting.

No, better not to think of that.

"How's it going?" Greyson says, coming up to me just as Yolan wanders off, apparently in search of more aloe vera cream.

I come to and realize I've been staring at Wynona unconsciously. She's on the dance floor with Josie and Sierra, now with Harley and Kyra too, and they're having so much fun it almost seems like an insult.

"Fine," I say, turning away. I waggle the drink in my hand. "This is only the second drink, you'll be happy to know."

He grunts, his gaze where mine was. "How is she?"

"Who?"

His icy blue gaze snaps to me. "You know."

"We really have to talk about it?" I ask.

Half the reason I told Greyson about Wynona all those years back was that he was the only brother I could trust not to tell the others. And the one who wouldn't badger me about it.

"Of course we don't," he says smoothly, running his hand through his dark tousled hair. "Not if it'll drive you to another drink."

I just scowl.

All I need to do is wait it out… but fuck it, talking about it won't hurt.

"She still hates me," I say.

"You expected any different?"

"Not really, just…" I scowl. "It took all my self-control not to go talk to her when we spotted her at the comedy club. Then, I thought maybe if things worked out with Mary…"

"Mary was insane," Greyson says very calmly.

"She was," I agree with a sigh. "But in the weeks after, and now my being here, it made me realize. I was only trying to make it work with her to get over Wynona. Same with the girls before her."

"Doesn't matter, though," I add. "What was between us is over. Wynona won't even talk to me now."

"Do you blame her?" Greyson asks.

I swing a look at him. "Aren't you supposed to be making me feel better?"

"Nope." He shrugs. "I'm supposed to distract you long enough to stop you from drinking yourself under the table."

I snort. "Thanks for the vote of confidence."

"There you are!" Harley says, wrapping her thin, tanned arms around Greyson, her sandy blonde waves dancing.

"You stole him from me," she accuses me with a winning smile.

I've always found Greyson's wife pretty and fun, although if she had darker hair and more tattoos, maybe…

"Guilty as charged," I say, already waving them away.

My phone rings again.

One glance and I'm gritting my teeth again, stalking off.

Picking it up, I say, "This had better be good."

CHAPTER 3

Wynona

"Okay, that's it," Sierra says, flopping down beside me. "I have" —she checks the sleek new iPhone Nolan bought her a few weeks ago— "about fifteen minutes until my husband and I will consummate our marriage."

As Josie giggles, Sierra continues, "First though, we've got as much alcohol as we need and as good a hiding spot as we'll get."

"Sitting behind the bar isn't exactly the world's best hiding spot," I point out.

"Nonsense," Sierra says firmly. "You wouldn't betray us, would you, Andrew?"

The bartender, a tall, tanned man with generous lips, turns around to wink and blow us a kiss. "Never, my pale princesses."

That sends us cracking up some more.

"Just tell her," Josie says, elbowing me with her stupid sparkly elbow.

I elbow her back. "No."

"I know, Wyn," Sierra says quietly.

"What?" I say.

"I figured it out years ago," she admits. "Found some pictures when you wanted me to see if I could retrieve all your old phone data. I didn't mean to look, they just came up, but—"

"And you never told me?" I ask, already reaching for the closest bottle. I guess some fruity sangria it is.

Sierra grabs it first, glaring at me. "I could say the same thing to you."

"Look. It was a painful part of my life. One I didn't want to recount. Anyway, that year, we were mad at each other because I'd messed up your birthday party, and I just… I don't know. I always planned to tell you. It just got further and further away. And eventually, it just seemed like it'd be just another terrible breakup for me to tell you about."

Sierra looks sad, really sad.

Jesus, I'm a crappy friend. And on her freaking wedding day, too!

But she's the one who brought it up.

"But when I started dating Nolan…" she says.

"I know," I say. "Jesus, I know. At first I just thought it'd blow over. It didn't seem like you two were serious. Then it seemed just, I don't know, too late?" I exhale. "Anyway, Emerson never introduced me to any of his family, so it can't have been that serious to him."

Josie raises her pink-sparkle-nailed hand. "Can I just say that I disagree?"

"You don't get a say," I growl, grabbing another nearby bottle and chugging it. "Ugh. What is this?"

"Malört," Josie says, chuckling. "And serves you right."

"Probably," I admit. "Sierra, I really am sorry. I felt terrible keeping it from you. The details of Him. The Big Breakup guy."

There's a silence.

Okay, not really a silence—not with Backstreet's Back playing in the background and Josie murmuring along under her breath, and someone's batty aunt yelling, "Piñata! Piñata!"—but a pause.

It's long enough to be worrying, not damning.

Sierra could still answer me, could still want to be my friend.

Hope isn't completely lost… right?

"Fine," she finally says. "Because I am a good person—and because I am drunk—and also because it is my wedding day, I will forgive you."

I hadn't even realized I was holding my breath until my exhale makes me drop the napkin I'd been aimlessly tearing into itty bitty pieces.

"But," Sierra continues, holding up the Malört bottle, "now for your punishment—"

"Bleaching her hair back strawberry blonde to match mine," Josie says eagerly.

I snort. "You just want to get out of visiting our doctor and have me go for you."

"Okay, the woman is scary," Josie grumbles. "A fact you yourself agreed on."

"She's a bully," I admit. "You just have to bully her back."

"Or get my twin to do it for me," Josie chirps. "Come on, it could be like the old days. We could live each other's lives."

"I don't want your life," I say flatly.

"Thanks a lot."

"I'd kill your plants in a week."

"Guys!" Sierra says loudly. "Hello? Bride speaking here? Now, as for your punishment, Wyn… I know just the thing."

"Wonderful," I say deadpan.

"Hey," she reminds me. "I was the one who was deceived for over five years, remember? Now, as for your punishment…" Eyeing me, she sighs. "Okay, fine, I'll take it easy on you. You just have to call a temporary truce with Emerson for the rest of the night. And not glare at him like you'd rather see him beheaded."

"Or run over by a truck several times," Josie chimes in helpfully.

"Aren't I supposed to be the morbid twin?" I point out.

She just shrugs. "Your wearing pink has me all mixed up."

"Do we have a deal?" Sierra says forcefully.

"Why do you even care?" I ask.

"Nolan mentioned that Emerson's been having a rough night," Sierra explains. "Anyway, you weren't there when he overdosed some months back."

"He what?!?" I find myself snapping with way more concern than I should.

"Never mind," I add quickly. "Don't tell me."

"Okay," Sierra says with a shrug, her gaze steady on me. "But we have a deal?"

"Depends." My gaze is steady back on her. "Am I allowed to say no?"

Sierra grins. "Nope."

The sound I make is part chuckle, part sigh. "Fine. Then sure. I won't glare daggers at him." I sigh again. "But I'm not going to go over there and make up, either."

Sierra nods, wobbling upright. "That's all I ask. As for me, I have a husband to dance with."

"You sure you don't want us to help you—" Josie begins, already half up.

"Nope," Sierra says firmly, placing the bottle beside us. "I'm drunk, but not so drunk that I can't make it across the dance floor. I love you. Goodbye."

We chuckle as she sashays off, albeit a little tipsily.

"She really seems happy," Josie says.

"She does," I agree. "I'm sure having a destination wedding on a tropical island helped."

"That and marrying the love of her life," Josie adds wistfully.

"Now, aren't you relieved you finally told her?" she says, turning her gaze my way.

"Yeah," I say. "I am. But do you know what tonight needs?"

She perks up beside me. "What?"

"Sleep," I say, getting up and offering her a hand.

"Sleep," Josie repeats slowly, as if the word might mean different things to each of us, staring at my hand without moving.

"Yep," I say, and catching her dumbfounded expression, I add, "I know, I know. Not exactly my normal MO, especially after a breakup. But as we both know, normal hasn't really been working out for me."

"Except as far as work, money, and dogs are concerned," Josie points out drily.

"You forgot my 'gymspertice', as you and Sierra call it," I shoot back just as drily. "But you know what I mean. I go through a breakup, then I drink and mope about until I get a new guy. Rinse and repeat. Maybe I'll keep doing that tomorrow, but right now, all I want is some sleep. And to go to bed before I'm so drunk off my face that I do something I'll regret."

"Like hook up with Emerson?" Josie quips.

"I was thinking more like kill my evil twin on the beach with the foul-tasting liquor," I say, hefting the bottle. "But that'll do."

Josie takes my hand. "I'd rather not die tonight. Nor have my death have any tie-in with the Worst Game Ever."

As we stroll along back to our rooms, I roll my eyes. "Overdramatic much?"

"Nope, just realistic. Clue was practically impossible to win!"

I can't help my self-satisfied smirk. "And yet I managed to, practically every time."

"Yeah, yeah." Josie stops. "Hold up. I'm gonna grab one more of those cupcakes you murdered for the road."

As she heads over to the banquet table, I glance around. The party is winding down. Sierra found Nolan, and they're slow dancing, forehead to forehead. Talk about couple's goals.

Even the music seems quieter, the crowd more somber.

One thing Josie used to say to me was that I always knew when to leave a party. Am I right in this case?

Part of me wants to stay, to have a fun, funny night to blot away my encounter with Emerson. But a bigger part of me is just plain tired.

Ahead of me, some guy with a handsome back surveys the crowd sadly.

He turns my way, and his eyes snap away.

Shit.

Of course.

Who else would have a handsome back other than Emerson Storm?

"It's okay," I call over just as he's turning away.

Mid-step, he freezes.

"We're on a truce," I call again, regretting it already.

With one step he swivels to face me, eyeing me like I'm a pipe bomb that could go off any second. "You're sure?"

He takes a few steps forward.

"No," I say with a chuckle, "but I don't want tonight ending on a bad note."

"You're going?" he says.

"To sleep." I nod. "Josie and I had a fun time, but it's time to turn in."

"Early flight tomorrow?" he says.

I shrug. "Not really."

He chuckles. "You're right. Even if you did, you'd probably get there on time. You always were good at that, I remember."

Catching my expression, he frowns. "Forget it."

"Okay," I say.

I swallow, craning to look around for Josie.

But damn the woman, she's found her new beau—the hot tall guy manning the food counter! Kill me.

"I shouldn't have followed you," he adds. "I get why you wouldn't want to talk to me."

"And yet, here you are," I say ruefully.

"Here I am." The start of what could be a smile. "Guess I'm just a glutton for punishment. Anyway, how are you? I heard you've got your own tattoo parlor now, a sweet crib."

"I'm not giving you a free tattoo," I say deadpan.

Catching on, Emerson purses his lips with frustration. "You didn't even let me pitch it to you. Imagine this—a dolphin, sitting on the Statue of Liberty, with a bong in the shape of Pingu."

We crack up at the same time.

"I can't take credit for that," Emerson admits. "Jared's brother got too trashed one night and got it done. And yeah, it's just as ugly as it sounds."

"Jared?" I say.

"A friend," he says, scanning the crowd. "Pretty sure he's off with some girl who works here, though. Kept trying to convince me to come along, that she had a sister or something."

I step back, sweeping my hand off. "Well. Don't let me stop you."

Something flickers in his eyes. Not hurt, but not indifference, either. "You're not."

"Okay."

"Okay."

I glance Josie's way again. She's laughing her head off at something he said while he's giving her what looks like a rose he got from somewhere?

Jesus.

At this rate, she's going to be having her own wedding by the end of the night.

"You're just the same, you know that?" Emerson says.

And suddenly, I remember what an idiot I'm being.

Maybe it's how buzzed I am or maybe it's how Sierra's 'truce' in my head makes it almost okay.

But I'm actually starting to be stupid enough to enjoy myself with him. And I may be stupid, but I'm not stupid enough to think that it would be anything but a bad idea.

"I should go," I say, already heading off.

"Hold on," Emerson says. "Maybe I shouldn't have—"

"No." I pause to look at him hard. "You shouldn't have. You don't know me anymore."

And as I walk off, it's with the satisfaction of knowing that as little as I might have changed in some ways, the old me would have stayed.

CHAPTER 4

Emerson

When I was under twenty, I'd never get hangovers.

I could glug down a third of a keg, guzzle so many cocktails I lost track, hell, race an equally drunken university linebacker and run smack into a stop sign, and come the next morning, I'd wake up as fresh as a babe.

Maybe that's why I have these habits. These old habits die hard.

I don't remember much about last night, but what I do remember after Wynona left involves a lot of drinks. A lot of drinks. Good thing Nolan turned in fairly early because he would've scolded me like Grandma Josephine back when she was in scolding condition.

I prop myself half-up, wincing.

Arôme de booze... is that really me? Fuck's sake, I'm cradling a bottle of tequila.

I push it away with a glare like it's to blame. Although, in a very legitimate way, it is.

It's official. I've got a splinter in my brain. What else could produce a headache so splitting?

These sheets may be Egyptian cotton as they claim—why do I know that?—but that doesn't stop them from being dirty. Almost like someone...

Why am I wearing my shoes in bed?

I sink back into the memory foam pillow, letting my eyes close.

I'd better see what pieces I can wrestle out of my memory bank before I venture out into the real world.

Okay, so there's Wynona not talking to me, which blew. Wynona talking to me, which was awesome. But then...

Fuck. I screwed up somehow.

She left.

More drinks egged the night on faster. I'm dancing. Jared's back with his girl.

A black blur tilts, and then I'm in my room, this room, chasing away some other girl. Who knows why?

Another black blur, and I'm on the beach alone, water up to my heels. Blur—my phone's going off—blur—and then—

I force myself half-upright again. Looks like that's as good as it's going to get, barring some wildcard memory of Wynona coming back.

More like a complete impossibility.

My cock twitches.

I glare at it.

Really? Semi-hard just from a stray thought of her?

My scowl deepens, but my erection doesn't go anywhere.

"Fuck it, might as well," I growl, grabbing it.

I close my eyes and let myself imagine how last night should've gone.

How she should've stayed and looked at me like she used to.

The intensity in those blue eyes I've never seemed to find anywhere else.

We would find our way onto the dance floor, into each other's arms. She'd fit in mine as perfectly as I remember.

Our bodies would move together, groove closer as seamlessly as two halves of a zipper. We'd get all tangled up.

Our mouths would find each other. Our tongues would play along.

I'd make caressing that tight body of hers into a dance move. She'd turn around and brush my cock with her ass as if it were just another move. As if she wasn't thinking, just then, exactly the same thing that I was.

Our eyes would meet.

Next thing we'd know, we'd be moving, leaving, on to the next part of the dance. The one that can't be avoided. That everything had always been leading up to.

The door would hardly be shut behind us when we'd be ripping off our clothes. She'd have more tattoos, pretty ones, swirling, hidden, like secrets for only me to see.

I would kiss her into the wall. She would press her body to mine like there weren't enough ways for her to touch me.

I'd cup her face and cover her mouth. She'd wrap her legs around me, her pink dress riding up.

My fingers would stray down. They'd get sidelined by her sweet little tits.

I'd part the V neckline of her dress into a U so that they popped out. They'd be the same pink-nipped upturned beauties that I'd dip my face into.

I'd inhale her scent, something incense-like and exotic and musky and dark all at once.

She'd groan "Emerson" over my shoulders. I'd lap her nipples nice and good.

My fingers would jag down, over her dress-clad torso, under the final part of the dress that had been shoved up.

They'd grasp toned thighs with just the right amount of meat on them. They'd grip her ass, so firm and fine. They'd snap the lacy band of her panties.

She'd smirk. I'd smirk.

"Go on," she'd say.

I'd go on. I'd more than go on.

I'd stroke that sweet pussy of hers, enjoying its contours. Then I'd delve deep inside it.

I'd flicker my fingers inside her until she sagged onto me, until, pulling out, I'd pick her up and toss her onto the bed.

She'd giggle, then groan.

I'd make her groan some more. A lot more.

"Just like that," she'd say, and she'd be right.

She needed it. We needed it.

Just like that.

I'd get her nice and wet and then I'd slip inside her.

Oh, fuck.

It would be just like before. Better than before.

Like coming home.

We'd hold each other tight, every part of us clasping the other. I would ram her so sweet and soft, she'd be cooing. I would ram her so wild and rough, she'd be begging for more.

"Please," she would groan, and that's all she'd need to say.

I'd take her legs and brace them on me so I could jackhammer her deep, so deep. So deep and fast and merciless that she would come again and again.

And I would come.

Yeah...

And my eyes would open and—

Instant disappointment. And disgust.

What the fuck was I thinking?

Don't I have a plane to catch?

Speaking of planes…

I grab my phone and… stare.

1:07 PM. That can't be right.

No.

No fucking way!

It can't be 1:07 PM because my flight leaves at 1:30 PM, which means…

"Shit!"

I race to the bathroom, throwing everything that looks like mine, and a few travel-size lotions, into my bag. Running around my room, I stub my toe once, almost throw the hotel's bible in my bag twice, and curse my brothers.

No one thought to check in on me?

By the time I get to the hotel lobby, I'm at a run. It's 1:12, and the airport is close, which means I could catch my plane…

But that's a really fucking big 'could'.

There's only one taxi.

I rip open the door. "Hey, I need to get to the airport STAT."

"Oh, sorry," I say, seeing someone in the back. "Is it okay if I…"

I trail off, gaping at who's sitting in the back seat, eyeing me coolly.

Out of all the fucking people…

"Get in," Wynona snaps.

"What?"

She grabs me and tugs me in.

"Go," she tells the driver.

As he takes off and Wynona turns away, I grumble, "Thanks."

"It's fine," she says, still keeping her gaze fixed outside her window. "I'm just late. Can't afford to be any later."

"You on the 1:30 flight back to NYC too?" I ask.

A pause.

Jesus fuck. This is the woman I just jerked off to.

"Yes," she says simply.

"Wonderful," I mutter under my breath.

The cab ride isn't the most enjoyable one I've ever taken.

While Wynona looks like some goth high-roller with her black velvet bomber coat, cherry-red lips, and big rhinestone sunglasses, my gaze keeps getting drawn to the sinister stain on my seat. Maybe it's because this car has a subtle smell, under some pretty powerful air freshener, of cat piss. The cabbie seems to think having windows opened as we race down the roaring highway constitutes air-conditioning. The beads of sweat forming at the nape of my neck seem to think otherwise.

The man manages to drive fast enough that the little legs of the hanging purple-skinned wooden hula girl on his dashboard jiggle, but not fast enough to get there in the 'five minutes to the airport' that the hotel brochure advertised.

We get there at 1:20. I let Wynona go to the airline counter first. I stay in line far enough back that I can't hear exactly what's being said, but whatever it is, it doesn't sound good.

When I see Wynona's black-nailed hands going up in exasperation, I head on over.

"Listen," I tell the airline stewardess, who might be pretty if her pencil-thin eyebrows weren't drawn into a don't-fuck-with-me expression. "There are still five minutes. Are you sure there isn't any way that we could—"

"No," she says flatly.

"Okay, drop me. Are you sure that you can't let my friend here" —I gesture to Wynona— "one more person on?"

"No," she says. "The plane is leaving. I'm sorry."

"You don't sound very sorry," Wynona says, arms crossed.

"You don't sound very sorry," I agree.

Wynona wilts with a sigh. "This is all my fault. I never should've taken that sleeping tablet. I just couldn't fall asleep, not after…" She trails off with a glare my way.

"Listen," I say, giving the airline stewardess my best smile, "there must be another plane soon. Tonight, perhaps?"

"I'll look," she says in an unoptimistic tone.

Two sips of the water bottle from the bar fridge in my room that I'm pretty sure the hotel is going to post-bill me for later, and she shakes her head. "None available today."

"Tomorrow then?" Wynona says, an edge in her voice.

Her water bottle is decorated with black and white cats that seem to be drawn Dali-style, although she doesn't touch it. She's busy on her phone.

Seeing her watering a fake flower on some phone game, I chuckle.

"What?" she snaps. "It's good for stress."

I make the wise choice not to say anything to that.

"None tomorrow," the airline stewardess chimes in, looking more pleased by the second.

Fuck.

Before Wynona can open her very angry-looking mouth, I say in the calmest voice I can muster, "Okay. When is the next flight, then?"

Seven more water sips later, and the woman nods. "A week."

"A week?" Wynona sputters. "But that's impossible."

"That's the earliest date," Evil Stewardess says.

"There's probably another airline with an earlier flight," I tell Wynona. "Let's go."

As it turns out, there isn't. We trudge on back to the original stewardess, buy ourselves some tickets, then catch the same taxi back to the same old hotel.

Talk about déjà vu.

"This is your fault," Wynona says about halfway through the taxi trip as the palm trees waggle in the wind outside.

"My fault?"

"Yes."

"Okay," I say.

There are not many ways that today could get worse, but fighting with Wynona in a cat-piss-stinking taxi would be one of them.

"If you hadn't played that song at the wedding reception and rattled me," she said, "then I'd have been able to sleep fine without a pill. I wouldn't have overslept."

"What do you want?" I snap. "For me to pay for your stupid extra plane ticket home? Fine. I'll do it."

There's a silence that I'm beginning to think might mean another truce, but then, voice dripping with disgust, Wynona says, "I don't want your money."

That's it.

"Listen," I growl, turning to her. "I didn't intend for that. I didn't intend for any of this. Why don't you take some responsibility for a goddamn change?"

"And why can't you leave me alone?" Wynona snaps. "Last night, your following me onto the beach like that—"

"Later, you said we had a truce," I say with as much patience as I can muster. Which just means that I'm not growling anymore.

"That was for Sierra," Wynona snaps. "Because she said—"

She stops suddenly, with a sullen glare my way.

"Oh, that's finally it?" I say sarcastically. "No more snapping at me?"

Head turned away, she says nothing.

"Fan-fucking-tastic," I snap, turning to my own window. "Suits me just fine."

The rest of the ride consists of bumping over a seemingly endless succession of potholes—the taxi driver took another route for whatever reason—listening to some Spanish singer croon out notes that indicate he's in entirely too good of a mood, and sticking my head out the window to get some respite from the heat.

When we get back, I go to the front desk and explain the situation. Turns out that Josie and Jeremy missed their flights too. Wynona's ready to beat it to the closest other hotel there is with Josie, but apparently, one of my brothers reamed out one of the concierges for not giving me a wake-up call as instructed, and they offer to let Wynona and me stay here for free until we can fly home.

So we go to our new separate rooms without a word.

Which, yeah, suits me just fine.

CHAPTER 5

Wynona

"Oh, God," is the first thing Josie says after I head to her room to wake her up and tell her the news.

"I know," I grumble.

"Oh God, oh God!"

"I know."

A long pause.

"Jesus, Wyn, I can't believe we both missed the flight," she continues. "You're just always the on-time one, and I just figured you'd wake me up and we'd get there just in time."

"It's fine," I grumble. "Completely fine. I'm just stuck here. In the same hotel as my ex."

"I guess at least it's free?" Josie says with a forced smile that convinces nobody, already trying to put a positive spin on things.

She's probably already had a few glorious dreams of rainbows, smiley frogs, and cute poufy dogs in the time I've been killing myself trying to make the stupid flight.

"There is that," I admit. "Anyway, I can just avoid him the whole time. Shouldn't be that hard."

"I'm sorry about last night, too," Josie says. "But if you had just talked to Antoine—"

"I much preferred my sleep, thanks," I reply. "What sleep I got, anyway. Jesus, I try to do the right thing for once, and look. It blows up in my face."

"At least you..." Josie's clearly searching here. "Still have your self-respect?"

"Hardly," I grumble. "I almost texted the lumberjack before calling you."

"You didn't," Josie gasps, hand flying to her mouth.

"I didn't actually do it," I clarify, "which is a good thing for me, I guess. But, you want to know the stupid part? I don't even want to talk to him."

Josie, to her credit, doesn't ask me who I do want to talk to.

"Would it be the worst thing," she says, "if you and Emerson were, you know, on neutral ground?"

I sigh, then roll my eyes at myself. I'm starting to feel like a Regency romance heroine with all the sighing and brooding I've been doing lately. Not that I'm exactly a Care Bear of joy and all things smiley back at home, either.

"Of course not," I admit. "I just don't think it's possible. Or safe."

"Fair," Josie says. "And at least I'm here, suffering with you?"

"True," I point out with the beginnings of a smile. "But thanks for the offer. Sierra offered to come visit too, but she's going on her honeymoon tomorrow, so I vetoed the hell out of that."

"To Thailand," Josie says on a sigh. "That girl has all the luck. Too bad we love her."

"Too bad, indeed," I say.

A knock sounds on her door. Josie answers it while I frown.

That had better not be who I'm worrying it is.

But it's just a concierge with some complimentary vanilla and chocolate cupcakes. Guess this island really has its cupcake game down.

"Yay!" Jose says with a happy bite of a chocolatey one, then sighs. "Guess we'll have to get Mom to look after Horatio and Maude, right?"

"True," I say.

"At least now you don't have to worry about me using your beloved antique cast-iron pan because I always screw it up." Her button nose scrunches in derision. "Jesus, Wynona, when did you become such a crotchety old woman?"

"Since forever?" I shoot back. "Don't you remember how when we were five, I'd hound you not to wear your shoes inside, even when our parents weren't there? And how for most of winter, I'd sit around under an afghan, drinking tea and knitting while the rest of you were out there tobogganing?"

Josie chuckles.

"Speaking of crotchety old women," I say, "I pretty much reamed out Emerson at the airport and in the taxi, even though he offered to pay for my new ticket."

"He did what?" Josie says.

"Don't," I grumble.

"I didn't say anything!" she protests. Her strawberry blonde ponytail bobs angrily while her oversized rubber duck pajamas ruffle a bit.

"You were going to," I say. "Anyway, maybe I was a bit of a bitch. But this whole situation is a bitch. A major mindfuck. I just want to be home watching some Cary Grant movie and—"

Another knock on the door

"Listen," Josie says, opening it, "We appreciate all this free food, but we'd really rather not... oh."

She swivels to give me a horrified smile. "Oh, Wynona?"

Seeing who's there, I quickly head out and tell Josie, "Five minutes."

Although if it's up to me, this will take less than two.

"Bye!" she sing-songs. "Talk later."

"Hey," Emerson says.

He looks handsome enough in a fitted blue T-shirt and jeans that talking to him for more than a minute probably isn't a good idea.

I cross my arms over my chest. "What do you want?"

His smile is neutral. "You wouldn't consider a sequel to our truce? Truce two?"

"Truce two," I reply flatly.

Emerson pauses for a few seconds, probably waiting for my unimpressed stare to lose its edge. It doesn't.

He turns away.

I should let him go.

On the spot, I can think of four different reasons I should—it will give me time to think over what I should do, I can use the time to read and calm down, he smells too good for it to be safe for me to be around him, I'm still attracted to him—and I'm sure there are about fifty more I could come up with if I had the time.

But I can't.

"Wait," I say.

He pauses.

"I'm sorry about before," I say, "blaming you for everything when it was my own fault I missed the flight. I was just frazzled. I've never missed a plane before, and..." I glare at him suspiciously. "Why are you smiling?"

His smile is rueful. "I just never thought you'd apologize. You seemed so sure of yourself, that I was in the wrong."

"Well, I have been determined over the past five years to hate you," I point out sweetly.

"And a stunning job you've done so far," Emerson returns easily. "I'd hate to kill your streak."

"Then don't," I say, flicking my chin back toward the hallway. "Leave me alone."

"We're in the same hotel."

"What do you want, Emerson?"

He meets my gaze, stare for stare. "It can't be to smooth things over so we don't glare every time we pass in the halls?"

"What do you want, Emerson?"

"To apologize."

"What do you want, Emerson?"

He scowls. "Fine. I was just thinking, if you did accept this truce and if you didn't completely hate me, then maybe you'd want to come along to the boat ride tonight."

I eye him. "What boat ride tonight?"

He chuckles. "You didn't even glance at the daily activity list handout in your room, did you?"

I didn't. "Why would I?"

"Because it's the only thing to do here?"

I recross my arms over my chest. "Well. Are you going to tell me what's on it tonight?"

"They're offering a free boat ride out on the bay to check out the dolphins."

"Oh."

"That's not a no," he points out.

I have to smile. "I'd have to be some kind of Satanist not to like dolphins."

Emerson's smirking himself. "Didn't you go through a phase where you hated ice cream?"

"Yeah, but that was because…" I trail off.

As easy as it is to forget myself with Emerson, I don't really know him all that well. Not anymore.

And I'm not about to admit to him that it was a stupid attempt to try losing weight to fit into this red sequined crop top for that Vegas House music festival we were all set to go to.

"I'll need to think about it," I tell Emerson.

"Fair," he says, turning away. Then he pauses. "If you don't want me there, I could skip it. Let you go yourself."

"I…" I swallow back the next words: Why are you being so nice to me?

Because really, I'm not sure I'm ready for the answer.

"Thanks," I say.

He leaves.

I stand there for longer than necessary before I head back to see Josie. She's back asleep though, lucky girl.

Inside my room, I do all the things I hadn't gotten around to doing yet. I put my clothes in the dresser and take out my toiletries. I finally take a look at that actually considerable activity list. I try to read.

But really, I'm done in less than twenty minutes, and I already know my answer.

CHAPTER 6

Emerson

"It's okay," I console Nolan over the phone. "Really."

"It's not okay!" His voice has enough vehemence for the both of us. "You got left at the hotel. With only Jeremy for company. And it has unlimited…"

He lets that part trail off, though we both know the word he's missing is 'booze'.

"I'll be fine," I tell him. "I went a bit hard last night, yeah. But honestly, that was a blip. And Jeremy isn't so bad, even if he isn't your favorite person."

"Honestly," he grumbles, "the man likes carrots more than is healthy. Plus, you're staying in the same hotel as your ex. That is not a recipe for good things."

"It's just a week."

"Disasters have brewed in less."

"As much as I appreciate your taking up the Grandma mantle," I tell him, "aren't you supposed to be getting ready for your honeymoon?"

"He is!" I hear Sierra further off.

"I have brotherly duties to attend to first," Nolan says stiffly.

"Well, consider them attended to," I tell him. "I'm fine."

"Just be careful, okay? I saw how you were looking at her."

I guess it was only a matter of time before Nolan found out that Wynona and I dated way back when. Although any night other than his wedding night would've been preferable.

I scowl. "It was a crazy night."

"Yeah, well, just make sure it doesn't turn into a crazy week."

"Didn't you used to be fun?" I quip.

"Marriage," Nolan says with a sigh. "It changes a man."

"Oh, don't you go pinning this on me!" I hear Sierra exclaim in the background.

"Yeah, well, this has been fun," I say.

"Emerson," Nolan says. "Seriously, just—"

"I know, I know," I cut him off. "Be careful. Okay. Bye."

"Emerson—"

I hang up, turning off my phone and tossing it onto the bed with a frown.

I know that Nolan's trying to do the right thing, checking up on me and looking out for me, but I'm really not in the mood.

My head's still messed up from last night and today, and the last thing I need to do is sit around thinking about it. I'm sure I'll have plenty of time for that when I get home.

Though really, it's probably better to put all this in that mental box that I don't look at.

The phone in my room goes off.

"I'm considering it," Wynona says as soon as I pick up.

"You called to tell me that?" I say.

"Fine." She sighs. "Let's do it. We can even try the truce thing too."

"Great."

"Great," she says. "Bye."

"Bye—" The phone beeps.

I frown, putting it down.

Guess I can't expect things to be great right away.

At any rate, I have—I check my phone—five more hours to eat and get ready.

I end up grabbing something to eat at the buffet, where there's no sign of Wynona. Then, a quick shower, which ends up not being as quick as expected.

She creeps into my thoughts at the most unexpected times—when I'm biting into a slice of cantaloupe at the buffet, while reaching for the shampoo in the shower...

Wonder what Wynona's doing right now?

I don't give myself time to answer that question. If I want any hope of keeping this truce intact, then I'm going to have to make damn sure that I don't cross that line.

But for fuck's sake, why is it that everything I want seems to be on the other side of it?

By the time I head over to the meeting place at the dock on the far right of the beach, the sun has started to set. Nearby, a beachside restaurant beckons with spicy rumba music and mouthwatering lamb and maki maki aromas.

In the crowd, she's not hard to spot. My cock hardens as soon as my eyes fall on her.

Trust Wynona not to make this easy on me. That intricately woven black crotchet cover-up she's wearing barely obscures her toned curves squeezed into a bright red bathing suit.

I head over, forcing my gaze off her ass. Even if it is a hella fine one.

Her paleness looks out of place, and her hair is in two shiny black balls on the sides of her head. Now doesn't seem like the time to want to kiss her.

"Imagine seeing you here." She whirls around in a flash, saying the words as she does so.

I blink. She giggles.

"I can smell you, you know," she takes great pleasure in informing me. "Same body spray."

I shrug. "Some things never change."

For some reason, that seems to annoy her, though she just shrugs back, saying, "And some things do."

Like you, I think but don't say.

Now that I'm here with her, I can see why what I said last night pissed her off.

There is something different about her. Though I'm fucked if I can put my finger on it. I can't pinpoint whether it's the way she carries herself, or the confident note in her speech, or something else.

"Had a good day?" I ask her.

She nods. "I managed to get everything back at home sorted. My Mom's going to look after my dogs. And my clients for the next week understood too—though a ten-percent discount helped. So that took a load off. Although I couldn't seem to wake up Josie. She's out to the world."

"I'm impressed that you actually went through with it," I tell her. "Setting up the business, I mean. I remember your making all those cool designs, taking the odd online course or two. But you actually went for it."

"You weren't such a terrible drawer yourself," she reminds me.

I shrug. "We were in a university drawing class. Greyson didn't want me only taking music classes."

"I remember," she says quietly.

I let the subject drop.

Out of all the things to tiptoe around, the class we met in should probably be one of them. Same goes for pretty much anything in our past... the past.

Although I can almost see it now... the black-haired girl who always wore those black studded boots. How I made myself ask her for a pencil that first time. Her purple-lipped smirk when she passed it to me, like she already knew where we were headed, what we'd become.

"Anyway," she says. "Building up my business was just what I felt like I had to do. Kind of like you and your music."

She shoots me a searching look, and I just nod.

Just then, the boatman starts loading people onto the boat, so we head on.

There are only a few other guests, so we get the pick of the boat. We choose a spot on the port side, a cubby that would be small enough for two if they sat close.

We sit as far apart as we can while staying in the same booth.

We sit there, her bare leg half an inch from mine. Her eyes are on the horizon. "It's beautiful. Even if we don't see any dolphins, this would be worth it."

The wind plays with her black hair, tosses the glossy strands around. The boatman shouts something to someone, then hits the motor.

The air still carries a hint of grilled lamb.

"I was so caught up in the wedding preparations with Josie, making sure everything was perfect for Sierra, that I didn't really take a second to enjoy it," Wynona says, still staring out at the water and beyond.

The blues of her eyes manage to be remote, awed, a bit sad at whatever they're seeing in that sunset.

She almost seems to be talking to herself as she continues, "So many things are like that. You rush through the best parts, just trying to get things done and done right, only realizing they were the best later. It's like we use memories to enjoy things, really. Though we're too late, of course."

Coming to, she gives her head a little shake and lets out a small chuckle. "God, I'm getting philosophical and I haven't even had any wine."

"I think the boat captain was offering some if you..." I trail off, seeing the slight downturn of her lips.

I follow her gaze.

She has a point, what she said.

I've spent several nights here, and not once have I noticed the sunset other than a fleeting two-second 'that's nice' thought.

Right now, a pink haze surrounds the half-sphere of the sun, a long swath of purple, then pink, on the horizon. It burns the waters into pale pink, broken by the navy swells of waves. The sky on the very edge looks bluer than I've ever seen.

"Maybe another week here isn't the worst thing," I say quietly.

Wynona glances at me, surprised. Her smile is rueful, almost naked-looking without her usual bold lipstick. "I don't know if I'd go that far."

I don't know what my smile is. "Come on. I can't be the worst ex you've had."

Wynona looks up to the left, pretending to tap her lip deep in thought.

I rip my gaze away. I'd like to cover that lip with something very different. Something that could ruin tonight within seconds.

"I don't know…" she says contemplatively. "I mean, there was this lumberjack who cheated on me with his second cousin, then tried to steal my dog, but then again, there was you…"

"Seriously?" I ask.

She chuckles, although her eyes haven't gotten the memo. "Guess I should've seen how he looked at that dog."

"Jesus, and I thought I was unlucky in love."

Her gaze swings my way, this time matching her frown. "Somehow, I doubt that."

I shrug. "Believe what you want. I won't go into details, but let's just say that my most recent ex is a first-class psycho."

Wynona quirks an eyebrow. "What is it they say about people who claim that every single one of their exes is insane?"

"Did I say every single one of mine was?" I find myself growling.

Her eyebrows lower. "I was joking."

"Fine," I say.

"Great," she says.

Already, the sunset is disappearing, its traces still on the left-behind waves.

Her question is so quiet that I almost don't hear it. "Is that what you said about me?"

"No." I turn her way, but she's not looking at me. "Of course not. I—"

"No," she says coolly. "You didn't even tell most of your brothers about me."

"Wynona, I—"

"No." She straightens, turning her back to me. "Forget it. I shouldn't have brought it up."

"No," I growl, turning away too. If she wants to play this game, then we can play it. "You shouldn't have."

The boat motor's still whirring, and we're gliding over the water at a good clip, spray flicking us every so often, when suddenly, the boatman cuts the motor. Now, we're riding the waves and seeing what we came here for.

"Look!" someone says.

I look, eyes skimming the waves, almost getting distracted by their lulling pulse until I see it. A rounded fin.

"Dolphins," Wynona murmurs.

Seconds later, the head belonging to the fin appears, a shiny bottle-neck dolphin with a grin that makes me grin too.

Another one pops out, then they make a whistling noise before disappearing under the surface.

"Must be your lucky night," the boatman says. "Not every day they visit us so close like this."

"I thought this is the dolphin sightseeing boat," a strident voice says.

"Lady," the boatman says, pursing his bulbous lips, "this tour is free."

We get a few more glimpses of the dolphins, heads popping up, swimming around, before the boatman starts the motor again.

During the ride back, the others chitchat among themselves easily, but not us. Wynona is still staring at the waves, her face lost in thought. Her shoulders are part-hunched, perhaps from the cool. Perhaps from me.

"Shit," Wynona says suddenly, lunging toward the side of the boat, reaching for something. I catch her just in time.

"What the hell were you doing?" I ask.

Wynona gapes at me, chest working hard, before she wrests herself away. She leans over the side of the boat, her gaze going to the water we just passed.

"My hat," she explains.

"So what?" I say. "You thought you'd just jump off the boat to get it?"

Her frown goes rueful. "I wasn't thinking." She turns my way, her smile grudging. "Thanks."

"You're welcome."

She doesn't say anything else the rest of the ride.

I think of a few things to say, about the color of the night sky, how it seems different from back home, or how the salty air has another scent that I can't place but maybe she could, or even about how the boatman's soundtrack this whole time has been nothing but Enrique Iglesias songs.

But it seems pointless, stupid, useless. Or at least unlikely to get that thoughtful frown off her face.

And then, all at once, we're back, getting off the boat.

"Thanks," Wynona says, not looking at me. "I should go."

I let her go without saying anything. She's a few steps away on the beach when I jog after her. "Wynona, wait!"

She waits, shoulders hunched, face twisted. "Don't, Emerson. Please. Just don't."

"I'm sorry," I say.

"You seem to be saying that a lot lately."

"Yeah, well, it's like you said," I find myself growling. "I don't know you. Not anymore. So, you can't expect me to know what will or won't set you off."

She considers this.

"I was an idiot before," I say. "I'm not asking you to give me a second chance. God knows I don't deserve that. Just—do we have to turn in already tonight?"

My gaze runs down the beach, looking for something, anything. "What about one of those cabanas?"

Her gaze follows mine. "What about it?"

"Want to check it out with me?" I say.

Her shoulders have relaxed and her face has untwisted into a thoughtful expression. "And if I said no?"

"Then I'd ask you why."

Her lips press together. "Hating you wouldn't be a good enough reason?"

"If it were true, maybe."

Her lips compress further. "Emerson."

That's it.

I turn on my heel. "Suit yourself." I storm over to the cabana.

I didn't really want to go here at all. I just suggested it for something to do.

But I'll be damned if I'm just going to slink back to my room to sulk. Or grab a drink, as much as I want to.

No sooner have I slung myself into one of the hammocks in the enclosure than I hear footsteps.

Wynona pokes her head in.

"It doesn't look bad," she admits.

I don't say anything.

She sighs. "I'm sorry, okay? I'm not exactly a garden of good vibes lately." Another sigh. "Jesus, who am I kidding? I've been a downer for years now." Her smile is sad, derisive, hollow. "I'm lucky my friends put up with me."

She turns away. "I'm sorry, Emerson. But I can't do this. I can't be around you and pretend that it doesn't hurt, that I've forgiven you. Because it does, and I haven't."

This time, I don't wait for her to take a few steps away before saying, "Wait."

She waits but doesn't turn.

"Please," she says quietly.

But the words are coming out of me, can't be stopped: "Just... I did it because I was hurting you."

She's shaking her head. "Please. Don't."

"Just listen to me, will you? I'm not asking for a second chance. I just want to explain. I always thought it'd be easier if I didn't, but now... I could see what long-distance was doing to you, Wynona. To us. I thought ending it would be easier and that maybe, with any luck, someday..."

She gapes at me. "But you said—"

"That I didn't feel it anymore, I know. I knew that if I told you the truth, you'd never accept it. But Jesus, Wyn, you were moping around at home, miserable, working at McDonald's part-time, and not trying for anything different."

She's shaking her head, a glare in her still-wide blue eyes. "Emerson. You said—"

"I know what I said, and I'm sorry." I grimace. "I know it's not enough. I know I don't deserve your forgiveness. But for tonight, please. Can we just sit here and look at the stars and maybe do that thing you talked about back on the boat today, the one where we enjoy the moment while it's happening, not after?"

Her mouth opens, then closes. Then opens. "I... don't know."

"Can we try?"

Slowly, gradually, her head moves into a nod, not looking at me. "Maybe."

And she sits there beside me, and I lean back, letting the hammock rock me back and forth, back and forth, back and...

Up above, the sky holds the kind of stars that city boys never get to see. They've got the brightness and numbers that you'd think were reserved for astronomers... or people on drugs. But they're here, now, these stars. They always were, these past few nights while we roved around, all busy with the wedding.

"Thank you," Wynona says softly, gazing up, face enrapt. "You were right."

"I can be. Sometimes." My smile is bitter. "Other times, I'm just a fool."

She doesn't answer, but she's probably right. Answering would just draw us back into it, away from what's here, what's now.

"Remember Cosmos?" Wynona says suddenly.

"Yeah."

She's turned to face me, her face almost hauntingly beautiful in the moonlight. Her eyes reflect the stars.

"Remember what he said, Neil deGrasse Tyson?" she murmurs. "'You, me, everyone...'"

"'We are made of star stuff,'" I chorus along with her.

Our eyes meet. Her blues in the dark are black, her pupils huge.

Now isn't the time, probably.

Yet, there are only two things that make me feel this way, so invigorated, so at home. Like I've finally found my place.

The first is music.

The second is where my lips are drawn right this instant, like a magnet.

CHAPTER 7

Wynona

"Emerson," I murmur into his lips, "I'm scared."

"I am too." He kisses me again.

And I don't know why on earth that makes it better, but it does.

His arms wrap around me. His hands grip me. As if he meant what he said and is already afraid of losing me. As if, like me, he's thinking now that anything this intense, this painfully real, can't be safe, can't last.

If it's too good to be true, then...

But he smells like that same Old Spice I hate on anyone else but him. And his lips are moving with mine with a rightness that makes me think, makes me remember...

Why everything fell apart when he left.

Maybe life is this big miracle, maybe we only need to remember that we are all star stuff, that there are so many things we still don't know, so many discoveries to make and wild, impossible things to achieve and see, but all I know is that I could never really believe in any of that, never really feel like that—like this—except with him. Life never felt like a miracle to me or anything but disappointing—except with him.

"Do you remember?" he murmurs in my ear.

My eyes flutter open and stare into his.

Those light blues hold that same unforgettable look. The one I always thought he saved for me, the one I later disbelieved in, was sure I'd made up.

A happiness greater than any he seemed capable of.

"I remember," he says.

And as his arms wrap around me and my body trembles with the rightness of it, I remember.

Oh, I remember.

Him, serenading me, a whole wheelbarrow of roses for Valentine's Day, outside my dorm window, grinning at the gaping girls and chuckling guys and hooting friends who wandered past.

Us, our first date in that little art café, and how he didn't invite me home, didn't even try. How he just drew me an ugly picture of an ostrich with the stub of a pencil on a lopsided napkin as we sat in some antique peg-legged, high-backed, scratchy-ass armchairs and talked and talked and talked while I waited for us to run out of things to say, only we never did.

That time we got too drunk on that expensive-but-terrible rum and some expired Fruitopia in my first shitty apartment, the one with the leaky ceiling and the neighbor with the fat greyhound that barked all day and night, and dog barking be damned, rain inside from the outside be damned, Emerson massaged my ass for a good two hours, stopping only to top up his rum-Fruitopia cup, entranced, murmuring, "Goddamn, Wynona. Goddamn, that ass," while I laughed whenever I wasn't moaning.

The time we showed up to that Hawaiian frat party head-to-toe done up as members of Kiss and convinced a few guys to let us do 'em up. How we rerouted the party to Josie's old place and filled the kiddie pool with so many drunk people it broke. How, after Emerson had promised to pay Josie, the two of us strolled down the street and he booked us a room in the nicest hotel just because. And we ordered meatballs from room service.

How I could tell Emerson's public smile from his real one—it was all in the lopsidedness of it for the real one, the one he saved almost exclusively for me.

But then was then, and now is now. The culmination of everything that happened in between.

"I can't do this anymore," he said that sunny afternoon over five years ago.

"This has to stop," he said.

I pull away.

One breath apart, one movement apart.

No.

I'm the one who can't do this. Not now.

I force myself out of the cabana, out onto the beach. I don't run, even though I want to.

But I don't pause, either. I walk, as slow and steady as the hand of a clock, as if my leaving is inevitable. As if I don't hear him behind me, back in the cabana, calling, "Wynona." As if every part of me didn't want me back in there with him, continuing what we started. As if we could really make it as though the past, the bad part of it, had never happened.

As my bare toes dig into the smooth half-wet sand on the shore and I wonder when exactly it was that I'd kicked off my sandals, I smile.

Maybe it's dangerous, being alone at night outside like this, but it's always been my favorite time.

Daytime is laden with expectations, watching eyes. Smile at the nice old lady. Don't hum to yourself or laugh at a joke in your head or do anything that could look too weird to anybody nearby. Don't stop too long to look at a rock, or the sky, or a tree, or anything like that, lest you look like a crazy fool.

Nighttime is different, at least when it's empty of people like this. I can walk fast or slow, or even backward. I can skip or just sit flat on my ass for no real reason at all, and the air won't make a peep. The sky won't widen its eyes. No, in nature, nothing I can do is unnatural except to cease existing.

"Wynona."

I sigh. I guess I couldn't really expect Emerson to stay back there, not after what happened.

"I'm sorry," he says.

I stop, letting him catch up. "I am too."

"I didn't mean for that to happen," he says.

I turn to look at him.

That sad, sad, beautiful man. The years have made him different, sure, but not in any of the ways that count.

He's still Emerson. The one I fell in love with.

"Don't you get it?" My voice sounds sad and weary, as though I'm some seer reciting preordained facts. "This is going to keep happening. We can't just pretend that the past never happened, that we can be friends."

"I know."

We look at each other.

"Maybe I don't want to be your friend," he finally says.

I look away. "Don't say that."

"It's the truth."

I turn to eye him. "So?"

"So, your turn."

"No." I shake my head. "It doesn't work like that."

"Why not?"

"Why not?" I almost laugh. "Because you don't get to dump me, long-distance, mind you, after three great years, and then stroll up over five years later and act as if nothing happened since. Okay?"

"That's not what I'm trying to—"

"Really? Because that's what it looks like to me, Emerson. If you'd bothered to ask."

I turn away and start walking. "Anyway, I'm not in a good place for anything right now."

"No?" He walks up alongside me.

"No."

"Why not?"

"Other than the fact that you messed things up all those years ago?"

His teeth grit. "Yeah."

"I'm going through a bad breakup."

"Oh."

As we continue along, nearing the hotel, I shoot him a skeptical sideways look. "That's it?"

He shrugs. "I went through one of those recently. I know what it's like."

"Do you?"

"It's bad," he admits. "Though I've had worse."

The way he looks at me as he says it confirms it. Asking him about that would be a bad, very bad idea.

"Yeah," I say quietly. "Me too."

I'm about to turn away when he says, "Did you ever see the new Cosmos? The one that came out this past year?"

I nod. "Wasn't as good."

And somewhere between his nodding and asking me a question about my tattoo business, we're locked in conversation again. And I know I should stop, that this is a slippery slope with fewer footholds the further we go, but I can't stop.

And at some point, my head has drifted onto his shoulder and my eyes have closed.

The next time they open, it's sunny and I'm in my own bed.

There's a knock on the door.

CHAPTER 8

Emerson

This is a dumbass idea.

She's not going to answer that door. I wouldn't answer that door if I were her.

I should just turn around, walk back to my room, and—

"Yeah?" The door opens a crack to show Wynona's sleepy blue eye.

"Hey," I say, lifting one of the plates in my hands. "Breakfast?"

"I…"

"I carried you back to your bed last night," I explain. "Hope that's okay."

The eye narrows—but then she nods. "All right."

When she opens the door further, though, she doesn't step away to let me in. Her half-smile is frozen, her eyes narrowed.

She eyes me for what seems like an age.

"I'm sorry if I was all over the place last night," she finally says.

"I'm sorry if I crossed the line, too," I say.

We look at each other as if deciding something.

She nods, then steps aside, letting me in.

There's something so timid about her right now, so beaten down, that a step into her room and I'm pausing again. "I can go, you know."

"What?"

"If my being here at this hotel is screwing it up for you, I could go to another one," I tell her.

Her stare goes flat. "You're serious."

I nod. "I've done enough to hurt you already."

She nods with a twist of a smile. "I get it. You're running away again."

"What? No, I—"

Her smile twists worse, once again naked-looking without that bright lipstick of hers that I'm so used to. "Yeah. Things get tough or complicated, and you peace out. Guess some things really haven't changed."

"Look," I snap, "I'm just trying to look out for you."

Her chin rises as she grabs the plate out of my hands. "Well, lucky for you, I'm perfectly capable of looking out for myself, thanks."

"Good," I snarl.

"Good," she snipes back.

We sling ourselves in the two suede armchairs in the corner of the room and start eating.

"So, when would you go?" she asks conversationally.

"As soon as I'm out of this room, if you want," I growl.

"I see."

"Right."

"And what do you want to do?" she asks.

I could throw my plate at the wall in frustration right about now. "This isn't about that."

She puts her fork down on her plate with an efficient clink as she aims her glare at me. "Well, it is for me. What do you want to do?"

Glare for glare, we sit there for a minute.

The effect of her eat-shit-and-die glare is somewhat diminished by the tiny crumb of bacon on the corner of her mouth.

Why now, of all times, do I want to brush that crumb away?

"I want to stay," I say.

"Okay," she says. "Then stay."

"Okay."

After a few minutes of silent eating, Wynona grudgingly admits, "You did good."

I almost smile. "Glad you still like a classic breakfast."

"I did have a vegan phase," she admits, "but it wasn't for me."

"Anyway," she continues before I have a chance to respond, "I should shower."

If that wasn't the cue for me to go—despite my cock perking up—then how she pointedly rises and looks to the door would be.

"See ya," I say.

"Bye," she says, closing the door.

I'm halfway down the hallway when I realize it.

Shit. While I was eating, I put my phone aside.

On Wynona's bed.

I race back, already cursing myself. Luckily for me, the door got caught on one of Wynona's sandals, so I let myself in.

I can hear the shower going.

"Just getting my phone," I call to her.

"What?" she calls, opening the door a crack.

My cock flexes.

Even just through a crack, the glimpse I get of her glistening curves is enough to make me instantly hard.

Goddamn.

"My phone," I say, lifting it.

I should look away.

I can't.

"What?" she asks in a voice that doesn't sound as annoyed as it should.

"Come here," I find myself saying.

She lets the door swing open further. "You first."

I don't need to be asked twice. I let my phone fall back onto the bed as I stride toward her.

Holy fuck. Would you just look at her?

Pale limbs perfectly toned, dark hair slicked back, lips pouted with an expression half-challenging, half-beckoning.

My lips land on hers, and the rest is what I've been wanting to do since I laid eyes on her. Before, even.

My hands slide all over her slick body, stroking the firm, supple flesh.

I kiss her lithe body into the wall.

Our lips seam together. Her tongue taunts mine, so I give her ass a little smack.

When she pulls away, her eyes are fire. "Yeah?"

"Yeah," I growl, and shove her mouth back to mine.

I take that tongue of hers and show her how it's going to be. How I like it. How she does.

My hands sweep down over her hips, and what I can't figure out is how I ever let her go.

She pulls off my belt. I undo my button. She kisses me into the wall, hands flat against my chest, taking as she wishes.

Now that's something new.

I reach over and give that fine ass of hers another good slap. She bites her lip and grins as a moan escapes her. I turn her around to get a better look.

"Jesus, Wynona," I growl, my hands finding their way to her slit.

It's wet, and not just with water.

I can't undo my pants fast enough. She rolls her hips and grinds her ass on my rock-hard erection as though dancing to a song only she can hear.

"Fuck, I missed this," I growl. "You."

"Emerson," she whines as my fingers play with her opening.

I pick her up and carry her over to the bed, tossing her onto it.

Next second, I'm stepping out of my pants, pinning her down, my fingers back inside her.

"Wet as fuck," I growl with approval as I move them inside her.

All Wynona can do is tilt back that gorgeous glossy head and moan.

Her slit is even tighter than I remembered, and already, my cock is itching to dip inside her. So I pull out my fingers and replace them with what she really wants in there.

Next second, she's crooning. "Whoa."

"Whoa," is all I can growl back, dipping deep inside her.

So warm. Wet. Tight.

So perfect for me.

I hold that first thrust deep in her for a good minute before I pull out partway again. Already, she's shaking, clasping onto me.

In I thrust, and out I pull. Deep and even deeper inside her.

"Yes," is all she can seem to say now.

I have to close my eyes. The image of her thrashing body, totally into it, is too much for me to take. I want to enjoy this as long as possible.

Our bodies move together with an ease that doesn't seem natural or real, with a rightness I'd almost forgotten or at the very least blotted away.

There's no ignoring what's going on now. The best sex I've ever had.

I gradually build my pace until I'm railing her with everything I have. She comes, crying out once, then again.

Then, when she loses it, louder and wilder than ever, I lose it too.

Afterward, drifting off, she looks gorgeous as hell passed out in my arms.

CHAPTER 9

Wynona

Huh.

I haven't felt this satisfied since…

My eyes snap open.

Oh, no. Oh, hell no.

I've had some crazy-realistic dreams. I've made my fair share of stupid mistakes.

But this?

No way. No fucking way.

I did not just sleep with Emerson Storm.

But the memory of his strong tanned arms, his tousled blond hair, hell, his smell which still lingers in my bed—there's no denying it.

I just fucking slept with Emerson Storm.

I woke up as peaceful and serene as if I were in Heaven. Now, the churning horror in my gut sends me straight to Hell.

How could I have done this? How could I have betrayed myself like this?

A single self-pitying tear streams down my cheek. I can't believe I didn't have enough self-respect to avoid sleeping with the man who broke my heart.

The only good thing about this is that I'm in my own room. I won't have to do a walk of shame down the hotel hallway.

Not that it matters. I've got a whole body full, a whole mind full of shame already, thank you very much.

I let the tears come, and soon, I'm sobbing in my bed like a complete train wreck.

Eventually, I collect myself and wipe away my tears.

Okay, Wynona, no time for a pity party. Think. There has to be something you can do other than scream-crying into your pillow.

But Jesus, this was the one thing, the one thing I swore to myself that I'd never let myself do. This was the one thing I'd prided myself on in the midst of so many relationship failures and weaknesses.

That I'd never gone crawling back to him. I'd never made that mistake again.

And here I am now, back in the thick of it, wandering down the hallway to the only place I can.

"Hey?" Josie says, opening the door.

"Sorry," I say. "It's early?"

"Early," she repeats groggily, still in the same pajamas. Yep, my sister has a gift for sleeping. "What's up?"

"Nothing," I say with a peppiness that even she is bound to see through. "Just thought that it might be nice to talk."

"Nice to talk?" Josie says, eyes blinking blearily. "Hmm. All right. Having fun?"

"Yep," I say. "I went on a boat ride and saw some dolphins last night."

"Dolphins!" That wakes her up. "Ugh, and I slept right through your trying to invite me, didn't I? They were super cute, weren't they?"

"Yes and yes," I tell her. "And the food here is really great, too."

"Awesome," she says. "Okay, I'm definitely not sleeping through tomorrow. And Emerson?"

I realize now that I've been standing up. I flop onto the bed.

God, what was I thinking, heading to Josie's room just now? As if I'd be able to blab on about the hotel without him coming up.

"Wynona?" Josie asks, a concerned note in her voice and eyes. "Is it hard?"

I swallow.

Say something, you idiot.

But I can't.

I can't lie to Josie. God, she's my twin, my sister. She'll see right through it even if she is hella sleepy.

"I... I just made a really big fucking mistake, Josie."

"Shit." Now she's completely awake. She opens the door wider. "Do you need to crash here?"

"Don't be ridiculous, I'll deal. I just—I can't believe I fell for it again. Made the exact same fucking mistake."

"Are you sure that it's a mistake?"

"Jesus, Josie, this is Emerson Storm we're talking about. He dumped me, and since then, not a word from him. And now he shows up acting all sorry and interested, and I just fall for it?"

Silence.

Even my cheery sister is clean out of cheery things to say.

"I'm a fool," I say before a ragged sob.

"Maybe he meant it?" Josie says quietly, her hand going to my arm.

"That's not the issue," I snap.

"Then what is?" Josie grumbles back. "If he really is sorry and interested and has changed, then what's the problem?"

"Don't you get it?" I say. "I can't trust him. Not after what he did. What happens the next time things get tough and he thinks he knows what's best for me and ends things again? I can't have my life turned upside-down by him again, Jos, I just can't. It took me too long and too much work to build up my life to where it is now. My business, my fitness, my finances. I'll be damned if I let some guy screw me over and ruin all that."

"But you don't have to—"

"Josie," I hiss. "You were there. You saw how I lost everything. Everything. My shitty job. The few friends I had left. My apartment. A year gone, spent moping around, hardly able to do anything. That was the legacy of Emerson Storm. That was what our breakup did to me."

"Not just that," Josie says quietly.

"What?"

"It wasn't just that," she argues. "Yeah, things went downhill for a year or so, but after that, Wynona, I'd never seen you so determined. Maybe you let your life be destroyed at first, what was left of it, but after that, you built it right back up, even better than before. You started your tattoo business. You went to the gym so often that Sierra and I started to worry. You got Maude."

"I can't afford to lose everything I worked so hard for," I insist.

"Then don't," Josie says. "If you're destined to lose your head over Emerson, then leave. Get out now, while you still can. But if you want to know what I think, Wyn, it's that you aren't the same girl you were back then. Your breakup with Emerson broke you, but it made you into a better person in the long run. I don't think you're going to lose everything. Not unless you let it happen."

Josie's words make sense. But the fear racing through my body, the tears rolling down my cheeks—they make their own kind of sense.

"I never told you this," Josie says quietly, "but he checked in on you, every few months, at least for the first few years. I didn't tell you because I knew it would just make things worse. But he never stopped caring about you, Wynona, at least not that I could see."

I sniffle. "Checking in to ease his guilty conscience. That's classic Emerson."

"But didn't he have a point?" Josie asks, her voice suddenly sharp. "Wyn, do you remember what you were like that last year when you and he were together and long-distance? You were irritable at everyone, hardly working. You hardly went out, wouldn't see friends. Maybe he was right to do what he did. Maybe it wasn't selfish, but selfless."

I sit there, staring ahead, waiting for Josie to come to her senses, to take it back.

"You don't mean that," I finally say.

"Wyn, I was there." Her voice is quiet but forceful. "I saw what you were like. Maybe at the beginning, your relationship was good for both of you, but by the end, you were a shell of yourself. I hate to say this, but—"

"Then don't," I interrupt her.

I know what's coming and want to avoid it with a self-preservation that may just be fear.

"Wyn." Her sleepy light blue eyes are narrowed in one of her rare no-nonsense moods. "You know I have a point."

"I know that right now, what I need is to vent," I grumble. "Didn't you tell me about some Instagram pic you saw from some spiritual influencer you didn't completely hate? Something about knowing when a friend needs a talking-to and when they need a shoulder to cry on? Well, right now, I need a shoulder to cry on."

Josie makes a skeptical noise. "Firstly, I'm your sister first, your friend second. And secondly, no, right now you need the truth. And the truth is that during that last year, you were a wreck. Being away from him and the inconsistent contact, and some of the pictures that were posted on Facebook... it all took its toll on you. Sure, Emerson did it in a shitty way, breaking up with you over the phone, but maybe it was the only way he could bear it."

So much for being a shoulder to cry on. Josie even skipped the whole 'talking to' part and just became a full-on the-truth-hurts sledgehammer straight to my heart.

The silence stretches.

From the window, a beam of sunlight stretches in like an outstretched arm.

"Just think about it," Josie says. "Or don't. God knows that being upbeat hasn't been your signature."

"No," I snap. "You took that all for yourself."

And before she can shut the door in exasperation, I stalk away back to my room.

Back in my room, I chuck my phone away in a pointless, feeble, half-hearted gesture. I don't want to bash it against the wall and break it. Not that I'm some winner of a thrower.

No, I'm petty, snapping at Josie for something she can't help. For as long as I can remember, my sister has been as cheery as I've been morose.

I give the phone a little kick for good measure, but I only manage to bash my big toe.

My big toe, with the ruby red polish still on. I painted them before I even arrived here, as I was wondering about the guest list and if he'd...

I turn on my side, then my belly, into the position I sleep in that's 'terrible for your body for seven different reasons', according to a WikiHow article I read.

As if I needed another reason to have a pity party for yours truly.

I lift my toes behind me and stretch the panging one. I fold my hands together in front of me and rest my head on them.

I consider the movement of my next tear.

Who am I, really?

Am I the capable woman who built her own business from the ground up, the one who kills it at the gym?

Or am I the wreck who can't keep a man, who's doomed to be alone for all time?

I roll around onto my back, quirking an ironic eyebrow even though I'm alone in this stupidly comfy room.

"Why can't I be both?" I wonder aloud.

The question seems more real, said aloud.

It's how I used to hype myself up after a breakup, talk myself in circles, say all sorts of ridiculous things into the open air, the kind of stuff you'd rather have a nail brutally yanked off than broadcast aloud to the public, like, "You are the strongest person I know," "You will get through this," "He will be sorry."

Right now, though, I don't feel strong. I'm not all that sure I'll get through this. Hell, I'm sure as shit that Emerson won't be sorry.

After all Josie told me, do I really want him to be?

The phone in my room rings.

I glare at it, at the seashell design on its back.

"Go away," I growl.

The phone rings out a reply, Not a chance.

I go to lie on my other side, staring into the wall. I stretch and flex my toe. It gives a good crack.

The phone rings and rings and rings and—

"Emerson," I snap, picking up, "not in the mood."

Silence.

Then, the sound of a dial tone.

My glare crumples into tears.

Before I had even made up my stupid mind, did I have to ruin everything?

He probably thinks I'm a psycho and is packing his bags already. As he's right to.

Unless...

I call him up.

Winner of The Most Bipolar Woman on the Island Award today goes to...

"Hi," he says flatly.

"Can we start over?" I ask tentatively. "Sorry, I've just been..." I trail off uselessly.

There are about fifteen words that come to mind, and none of them is the right one.

"All right," he says. "I've just been… too."

I frown. "You making fun of me?"

"Not really. I get it. Last night was a mindfuck."

I've been pressing the tiny half-moons of my nails into my palm.

Is he hinting at what I think he is?

"Meaning?"

"Meaning I get why you'd be freaked."

"So, you're freaked."

"I've had better mornings," he says shortly.

"Oh."

He exhales. "Jesus, Wynona, I woke up and didn't know what to do, so I left. Then, I call you up and—"

"I know, and I'm sorry," I say. "I just… didn't expect this. It's a lot to process."

"That's putting it mildly," he says.

A pause, then he says, "But I can see you again?"

I manage to chuckle. "You sure you want to?"

He chuckles too. "If your snapping at me every morning is the worst of it, then I think I can handle it."

"Oh, you haven't seen the worst yet," I reply smoothly. "Believe me."

"Is that a threat?" His rolling baritone is light, amused.

"Just want you to know what you're in for," I say sweetly.

"I already knew you were a handful."

"Thanks," I say sarcastically.

"The kind of handful I like."

"Ooh, smooth," I quip. "Is this the part where I invite you over and casually mention that I'm in my pajamas and still in bed?"

"Now that you mention it…"

"Can I just have some time?" I'm surprised to hear myself say in a more or less steady voice. As soon as I heard Emerson's voice, my first instinct was to want to see the handsome tanned square of a face that it belonged to, but that might not be the best thing right now. "To think. I just finished talking with Josie."

"Fair," Emerson says. "How much time?"

"A few hours, at least."

"Perfect," he returns smoothly. "Then you can make dinner tonight."

I find myself chuckling again. Emerson does seem to have that effect on me. "You couldn't wait to ask me for a few hours?"

"Bad idea," he says. "Wait that long and you could have plans already."

"Yes," I quip. "With all the appealing hermit crabs on the beach, who knows how long my nights will stay free?"

"That a yes?"

"It's not a no," I say.

"Wynona—"

"I'll keep tonight open for you and think," I say. "I'll let you know in a few hours."

"All right," he says. "In a few hours, then."

Turns out it's not a few hours. It's one.

One hour of doing an online yoga routine with Josie and an instructor whose patronizing nasal voice makes me want to strangle her, which somewhat mars the calm from the poses. I manage to finish it anyway, although certain poses—downward dog and warrior two, to name a couple, feel... overtly sexual in light of last night.

Or maybe it's just me.

Obviously, I haven't been a cloistered nun for the five years Emerson and I have been apart. But there's sex, and then there's... sex.

The kind of sex you glimpse in movies and sometimes even porn. The kind that's so good that it seems mythical, like a flying pig or a Neanderthal.

The kind that I'd once had. The kind that, before last night, I thought I was remembering with nostalgia's rosy glasses, overblown and overdone in my inexperience.

But now? Now I know.

It was just as good as I remembered—better, even.

Spontaneous, perfect, easy.

Like two dancers who had been away for years, returning for their signature dance.

I force myself upright from savasana, the final resting pose of my yoga practice, where I've evidently let my mind wander.

Problem is, is the insanely good sex clouding my judgment?

Or is it the misguided hope of righting old wrongs, the kind that can't be righted?

After Josie heads to the buffet, I take a quick shower first, with how sweaty and icky I feel. Inside the pretty-tiled shower, I amuse myself with how much I can bend the showerhead around, even if, in my scatterbrained state—I wonder where Emerson was thinking for tonight—I end up spraying myself in the face with the steady spurts of hot water.

Brilliant, Wynona. Just brilliant.

Only once I've toweled myself off, slurped out the small remainder of my purple hibiscus-smelling hairstyling mousse and chosen a comfy flowing peach dress that Josie bought me here, which I never thought I'd actually wear, do I feel anything near grounded.

"Okay," I tell my reflection. "You can do this."

Even she doesn't look so sure.

At any rate, I find Emerson where I expect to, at the buffet. Josie's long gone, her text—gone beach-walking, give Emerson a chance!!! ;)—making me smile and frown too.

Emerson waves me down, and I stop by to tell him, "Tonight works."

As I turn away, he calls, "Wait."

I pause.

"That's it?" he asks, eyeing me and the flows of the peach dress on my body.

Keep your cool, Wyn.

I flick my head to the side. "Just grabbing some food."

Emerson moves his sun hat off the seat next to him. "I've saved you a spot."

"Thanks, but I'm doing the in-room thing," I tell him. "See you later."

I'm a few steps away, heart beating as fast and insistently as a drill, when he says, "Wynona?"

I pause and look over my shoulder at him.

"See you later," he says, and I smile.

I keep my victory dance until I'm alone in my room again.

With two hash browns stabbed on my fork for a microphone, I sing along and shake my hips to Diana Ross's I'm Coming Out.

Why?

Because, ladies and gentlemen, Wynona Cowell kept her cool with Emerson Storm.

And it feels damn good.

Maybe this whole thing didn't start on my terms. But that doesn't mean it can't continue on them.

A couple of hours later, Emerson calls and tells me the time and place—6:00 PM at that nice beachside restaurant we passed when boarding the boat. Then I argue with Josie over why Emerson and I should have a double-date with her and Antoine, which she quashes with a simple Neither of us are there yet. That decided, we go over which dress I should wear.

She's all for the flowy peach one I'm already wearing. "That way, you can eat like food triplets and be A-okay."

I push for the red- and black-panel bandage dress. "It's so tight, it'll allow no food babies, so I won't overeat, so there's no chance of getting those stomachaches I get sometimes when I stuff myself."

Josie just snorts and accuses those stomach pains of being an 'urban legend' and an excuse for me to get out of shit I didn't want to do, and she may have a point, although I legitimately do get them at times.

At any rate, by the time Josie has left for her own date and I've sucked my belly and ass in enough to yank over the horrendously tight red and black bandage dress, added some charcoal black-winged liner and deep ruby-red lips, plucked stray eyebrow hairs that seemingly popped up overnight, chosen my second-best pair of black suede heels—the best black patent leather ones having a bad crack in them I hadn't noticed before—and raced outside, Emerson has been waiting there for at least fifteen minutes.

"I'm sorry," I start. "I left, then realized I'd forgotten my purse, then—"

Emerson's hand catches mine, though all he has eyes for is my body, following the lines of the dress as if he were the red and black panels himself. "No worries."

I grin, biting my lip, then inwardly curse.

Damn it—my lipstick!

Red stains on your teeth do not a sexy vixen make.

"Not even a few?" I quip.

He purses his lips and narrows his eyes, his typical 'alpha man' face we used to giggle about back in the day. "We'll see."

And then he leads me along, hand in hand, down the beach. "Good day?"

"Relaxing," I say. "And you?"

He shrugs. "Got to play on my keyboard a bit."

As we walk, the rich aromas of roast lamb and vegetables are growing stronger, like a welcome banner.

"You really still love it, don't you?" I ask.

"Yeah. I do."

"Good," I say, and I'm surprised I mean it. Back before, with piano being a huge part of what I saw as breaking us up, I hated it, resented it. "I've never seen you happier than when you play."

His sandy eyebrows rise and those blue eyes go to me. "Never?"

"All right." Boy, can he make me smile. "Almost never."

"We Storm boys stick to things," he says, almost to himself.

I'm not sure what to say to that other than the truth, that it makes my heart jump... and then fall with a stutter. So, I don't say anything.

Besides, we're here.

Here is a bus-sized wicker-floor patio with cushioned wicker chairs and tables with cheery blooms of red and orange hibiscus in vases in the center. It's set in front of a tiny building emitting not just that literally mouthwatering smell but also conga drum music that has my hips twitching to shake.

The owner, a tanned bald man with a smile so white it's almost painful to look at, strides up to us in a hibiscus-print purple and white button-up shirt, white knee-length denim shorts, and tan Birkenstocks.

"Reservation for Mr. Storm? Good to have you." He turns around and gestures to us with a sun-spotted arm to follow. "Never before had someone booking the whole place." He pauses to wink. "Less work for me."

We sit at the table he gestures at, and as he wanders off, I look to Emerson. "You did what?"

He shrugs. "This place sits twenty tops. Wasn't a big deal."

"But you didn't have to do that! And why?"

Another shrug of those big manly shoulders that I know look even better out of a shirt. "I wanted tonight to be special. Figured I owed you that at the very least."

I eye him.

Is it messed up that when someone says exactly-to-the-word what I would've wanted them to, that my first instinct is to be suspicious?

Emerson's already picking up the menu, completely oblivious of my scrutiny.

Typical boy.

For that matter, the only time he noticed that I changed my hair was when I went from black to pink.

"Thoughts?" he asks from his menu.

A long, searching look at mine, and all I can come up with is "Not sure."

Emerson makes a dissatisfied noise. "Everything looks good is the damn problem. But what I'm smelling..."

"The lamb," I agree with an excited nod.

"Hell yeah," he agrees.

Our eyes meet.

"Great minds think alike," he quips.

God, his eyes are pretty.

But not too pretty, like the star of some CW teen drama. Just the right blend of pretty and rugged, that baby blue color but narrowed atop high cheekbones. Like a Swedish model who might have had Viking ancestors.

His chair scrapes across the floor as he moves it right next to mine.

I have to laugh. "Seriously?"

He leans over to kiss into my ear. "Seriously."

"We're going to look like that couple?" I ask.

He shrugs. "Why not? Anyone you're worried about making a bad impression on?"

"No," I admit. "But..."

Emerson makes a face. "Most times I've been annoyed or weirded out by 'that couple', it's because I've been feeling lonely or bad about something else. Otherwise, why the hell would I give a damn about someone else and their PDA?"

"But when it's over the top, it's just rude." I scrunch up my nose. "Gross, even."

"Okay, I'm not talking about fingering on the dance floor," Emerson says with a chuckle. "But just a long hug, or sitting side by side at a restaurant? Who the hell cares?"

His easy smile brings mine as swiftly as a snap.

"You know, you're right," I tell him.

"I usually am," he says offhandedly in a cocky voice that makes us both laugh.

"You two look like you're having a good night," the owner says, returning.

"We are." I find myself feeling stupid with how much I mean it and how big my smile is.

Yep, we're one of 'those couples', all right.

"I'm Bob, by the way," the man continues. "Owned this place going on twenty years now, and I have to say, it's rare I see two people in love like you two."

Cue the awkward silence.

Because we are way far from saying 'I love you' to each other. We're still at the point where we don't even really talk about where or what we are, it's so nebulous.

Close up, Bob smells like clean laundry.

Emerson clears his throat. "We'd like the lamb. Smells delicious."

Bob nods his stubbled double chins judiciously. "It is delicious. I was making some for myself, actually, but I can have that be yours first. Shouldn't be eating on the job, anyway."

"You're sure?" I ask.

But he's already nodding, hurrying off. "Two lambs coming right up! With a lotta those grilled veggies!"

I look to Emerson, then beyond.

Clearly, I am starving, since as far as I can see, the setting sun has baked the sky into a rosy pastry. Every pinky-red line of the reflecting waves below could just as easily be a crease in the dough.

"Tell me more," Emerson says suddenly, and I glance at him, startled.

His eyes are on the same rosy horizon, although his monotoned words are for me. "You were right before. I don't really know you. But I want to."

I aim an undecided smile at him, resisting the urge to fiddle with my fork. "And my reciting facts at you would change that?"

"Telling me more means reciting facts at me?" he returns easily.

"No," I admit. "Though 'tell me more' is a vague request."

He inclines his head in agreement. "Fine. Tell me more about you, your business, your dog."

"Dogs," I correct him. "I inherited Sierra's dog Horatio after she was having trouble. To be fair, he wasn't the best dog to begin with, but now that we've potty-trained him, that's a step. As for my business, I'd say I've built up a pretty solid client base. Some weeks are busier than others, but that gives me time for a breather too. Although I do love it."

Emerson takes my hand. "I'd like to see you at work sometime."

"That's easy." I grin at him. "Just get some cliché quote on your arm, and it's done."

Emerson frowns. "You think I'd want something like that?"

Shrugging one shoulder makes my red dress strap slip down. I adjust it. "Everyone gets cliché quotes. The only thing I judge are those funny tattoo fails online—the ones with hideous pictures or misspelled quotes that mean something like 'eat shit and die' in another language."

We both chuckle at that.

"Any favorites?" he asks.

"A few," I admit. "I really like the watercolor tattoos, how they turn out, even if they don't last well."

"Some of the best things don't," Emerson says, frowning again for a period to his sentence.

I fall silent myself.

Is he wondering, same as me, if we belong to that class of 'best things'?

Or maybe I'm just being paranoid.

Probably.

Back when we were kids, and Josie and I loved roller coasters, she'd ride on them screaming while I'd be swearing that 'we're all gonna die.' I'm not sure when jumping to the worst conclusion became my MO, but somewhere along the way, it did.

"What about you?" I find myself saying, mid-fork-fiddle. "What's life like for the Emerson Storm?"

Emerson snorts. "Now you're just making me sound like a tool. I get gigs here and there. Life has been a bit chaotic lately, with all the scandals Dad's company and my brothers have been through. And Dad's passing away, of course. Plus, every one of my brothers getting married."

"I miss Dad like crazy," he continues. "Barely get to talk to Mom, either. It makes you wonder."

"Oh, yeah?" I say, putting my fork down and looking at him.

He pauses, brow creasing, as if he were half talking to himself.

"They were so in love," he says, his narrowed eyes still not meeting mine. Almost as if he's seeing small marionettes of them acting out the whole thing on the adjacent table. "So good together. Dad was expansive, Mom was cautious. They brought out the best in each other, and then…"

He shakes his head. "I'm being stupid."

"No," I protest.

"I am," he declares, a frown forming around the words. He picks up the clouded glass of water I hadn't even noticed on the table, then puts it down, still frowning. "I'm talking about them as if I knew them, as if I were more than six when they broke up." His shoulders shift with a restless movement. "All I really know about them I heard from Dad when he got drunk with me one time years back and was in a wistful mood. God knows, he was always a romantic when he was plastered."

He looks at me head-on, his gaze suddenly as lucid and sharp as a penknife. "He cheated on her, you know. Dozens of times. It was when things were going bad, but still. That was what did it in the end. That was what broke her heart. Now, she can't even visit us without it hurting more."

I reach for his hand, a tensed claw on the tabletop. "I'm sorry."

He lets me take it, although his hand doesn't relax with the contact. It's like holding a marble sculpture of a hand.

"It's fine," he says. "That's another way we learn, right? From our parents' mistakes."

I nod, since what he said is one of those limp truisms that sound true.

His allusion brings to mind my own parents, the quintessential 'good' parents, still in love, good-natured, and caring. And yet utterly foreign to me.

They've been baffled since I was four and wasn't like perfectly well-adjusted Josie. I think they still aren't quite so sure of what to make of me.

"I think we have to be careful," I find myself saying, "that in avoiding making past mistakes—whether our parents' our ours—we don't make more in turn."

Emerson eyes me. "Now, that sounds like a riddle."

"I don't know," I say, talking to the water, now only hazed with the last of pink amid a swath of indifferent navy from the sky above. "It's always seemed to me that by people saying that 'relationships are too much work' and 'not worth it', they're just avoiding being hurt. They're just scared. Sure, sometimes they might have some avant-garde reason for it, defying stereotypes and such, and that's not to say that there aren't other ways to be happy, just…" I trail off, chuckling. "I don't know what I'm saying. Forget it."

Emerson is looking at me curiously, but he nods, eyes focused past me.

On the dinner coming our way.

We eat our lamb in a comfortable silence. It's so good that taking my mind off it for half a second seems sacrilegious.

And yet, I do.

I wonder at myself. Why I'm like this with him, going off on these pseudo-philosophical tangents.

Why?

I swallow a too-big piece of lamb in my anxious reverie and end up cough-choking on it before finally washing it down with a huge gulp of water.

Gelato that cools my tongue with rich minty decadence is dessert. We argue over the bill, and he insists on getting it. "After all, I was the one who invited you."

"Beach walk?" Emerson offers as we rise to go, but I shake my head.

"I think I'll… turn in. Everything's happened so fast that… slow might be good. For tonight, at least."

Emerson pauses, his disappointed frown contrasting with the blank eyes he turns on me. "Yeah?"

I turn my head and nod. "Yeah."

Emerson doesn't mention how it's only nine o'clock. He doesn't mention how, tonight, the hotel activity program delivered into our rooms had at least three worthwhile activities—a comedy show, a bonfire, and stargazing. Instead, he takes my hand and says, "I'll walk you, then."

As we walk along, I can't help a "That's it?" from slipping out.

An ironic look. "You'd rather I argue?"

"No." I laugh a little. "I just figured—"

"That I'd pressure you?" He gives his head a small shake as we continue on, into the violently air-conditioned hotel lobby with star-shaped black and white tiles.

"Not exactly," I admit.

We lapse into silence as we venture in further, passing lazily pleased-looking hotel guests making their way to their rooms or the bar. His hand in mine is as steady and right-fitting as a mitten.

At my door, we pause.

No sooner has the question—Will he?—entered my mind than he is, his lips landing on mine. His kiss is an answer and a question, a leading and a straying. He kisses me like his lips want to say what's been unsaid this whole time, whatever it is.

He's the one to pull away, though, and we stand there with our faces close, breathing hard.

In an abrupt motion, he jolts himself away, tearing his gaze off my lips, off me.

"I'll respect your wishes," he says.

"Thank you," I say.

"Goodnight."

"Goodnight."

We stand there, looking at each other, daring the other to make the final move.

It doesn't help that Emerson is stupidly, ridiculously gorgeous. That tousled blond hair, those blue eyes, that sculpted jawline that magazines would pay good money for. His massive hulking shoulders and arms, the sculpted six-pack-clad torso that I know looks even better naked.

"Goodbye," Emerson says again, this time more for himself than for me, turning away.

And it's a good thing that he leaves since I couldn't hold it in any longer. There's this physical want in me, as intrinsic and basic as a gnawing itch, a piercing toothache, to press myself against him and let our bodies do the rest.

Seconds later, though, he's striding back. "Wynona, there's one more thing I want you to know."

A phone rings.

We freeze.

Emerson scowls, hand going instinctively to his leather coat pocket. Then he shakes his head and drops his hand again.

"You should get that," I tell him.

"It's fine. Really, it's fine," I tell him.

Scowling, he picks it up, then, seeing the caller, his scowl deepens.

"I have to take this," he growls, stalking off.

I watch him go, wondering who it could possibly be.

CHAPTER 10

Emerson

"This had better be good," I tell her back in the lobby.

To think I strode right by her minutes ago, was so engrossed with Wynona that I didn't even notice.

Now, though, there's no escaping her.

Mary looks at me, teary eyes wide yet narrow at the same time. Not believing what they're seeing. Not liking it one bit.

"That's it?" she asks quietly.

That same husky voice that could carry a tune ridiculously well.

She's done something different with her hair, cut it or something, but she's all the same. Same pretty olive-skinned oval of a face, brown eyes, dyed blonde hair. That cute mole on her chin is still there. Her nervous smile shows tiny little teeth like a rabbit.

"What do you want me to say?" I ask her in a low voice. "I didn't ask you to come here."

"No," she says slowly. "But you did ask for another chance."

I eye her. "Yeah, half a year ago."

"I..." She trails off, eyes finally narrowing. "Wow. You're really still bitter, aren't you?"

"That you dumped me with no explanation, nothing but a 'goodbye' text out of the blue? No, actually."

It seems too cruel to admit the full truth of it. When I look at you now, I feel nothing.

"Then what is it?" she asks.

She takes a step forward, and her same perfume washes over me—like clean rain on a summer day.

Next thing I know, she's wrapped her arms around me, murmuring, "Tell me, Emerson. Do you really feel nothing now?"

The answer is a resounding 'yes', but as calm as Mary is now, I know things can quickly turn bad. I'm not in the mood for a public scene.

So, I start an internal count to five. One… two… three…

"Seriously?" a horribly familiar voice says.

I rip myself free to see Wynona, arms crossed as she looks at me, smiling the worst smile possible. "Wow. I should've figured, right?"

"It's not what you think—" I begin.

Mary grabs my arm. I rip myself free. "Wynona."

Her upper lip is curled. "This was a mistake."

And as she strides off, all I can think is understatement of the fucking century.

"Who the hell was that?" Mary demands, rounding on me with her little cleft chin shoved out.

For the first time, I notice she's in an outfit I would've gone wild over before, denim cut-offs with a little beaded crop top.

"We're broken-up," I tell her flatly. "Remember?"

"Emerson," she says, grabbing my arm. "Please, just—"

"There's someone else, okay?" I say, stepping away.

She deflates, staring at me.

"It's her," she says finally, quietly. "Isn't it?"

"What are you talking about?" I ask.

As much as I feel for Mary, what I really need to do right now is get to Wynona and explain.

"That girl, it was her," Mary says, tangerine upper lip trembling. Her eyes burn. "You want to know why I dumped you with no explanation? Because one night, blackout drunk, you confessed to me that you'd only ever been in love once but that you'd screwed it up and lost her forever."

"I said that?"

She twitches as if she's been struck. "So, it's true then?"

I look at her sadly. "I'm sorry."

"You're sorry?" She laughs. "That's it?"

"I never meant to hurt you," I say.

"Well, you did, so screw you," she says, storming off a few steps, then pausing.

"What?" I ask.

"I booked a night here," she confesses. Then her mouth contorts into a snarl. "But don't worry, I'll stay out of your way."

I watch her go, trying to think of something to say.

But there isn't much that would do any good. 'Sorry' just about covers it.

And if I were in Mary's situation, I wouldn't want me to make it better. I'd want me to tell the truth, as painful as it is.

I head down the hallway to Wynona's room.

I don't expect her to answer when I knock the first time, but I try it anyway.

One knock... two... three...

"C'mon," I say through the door. "Just give me a chance to explain."

"No need," she replies. "I release you. You can go back to her. I should've expected something like this."

A maid passing by with her cleaning dolly shoots me a sympathetic look. I give her a tight move-along smile.

"Wynona," I find myself growling. "First misunderstanding we have and you jump to the worst conclusion? That girl could've been an old friend."

She pauses. "Friends don't hug like that."

"Open the door, Wynona."

Silence.

"Wynona!"

"No."

"Open the door."

"No. I won't."

I lean against the door, breathing hard.

"Just go away," she grumbles.

I sit down. "Why won't you just let me explain?"

A pause. "I'm not in a good place to talk over anything."

I think of the many responses for this. None of them will do the trick.

"All right," I say.

And then I leave.

Back at my room is the same sympathetic maid.

"I let her in," she says with a suggestive smile.

"What?" I say.

She just winks. "You'll see."

Yeah, 10/10 I'm not going to like this.

I tear open the door and lock it behind me. The last thing I need is Wynona changing her mind and deciding now's the time to storm in.

Yeah... it's as bad as I thought. Mary's sitting on the bed, her beady top and tiny shorts off and nothing underneath.

"I just want it to be how it was before," she says, rising. "Let's just pretend the past few months never happened."

I keep my gaze on the wall. "We can't do that, Mary. I'm sorry."

"Just once... for old time's sake?"

I shake my head. "Can't you see that this woman means everything to me?" I exhale. "I am sorry, Mary. But you need to go."

"Emerson—"

"I never meant to hurt you," I say quietly.

A minute passes.

Maybe she's waiting for me to change my mind. But the thought never so much as enters my head.

Yeah, I believe in second chances, and yeah, if Wynona wasn't here, maybe I'd even give Mary a second chance.

But this is my second chance, and I have no plans on messing it up. And Mary deserves better than being second-best.

"And yet, you keep doing just that," she says bitterly before dressing and storming out.

I stand there for a few seconds, looking at the door she slammed shut behind her. Then, I do the only thing I'm drawn to. I take out my keyboard and start to play.

At first, it's just random notes, smatterings of sad, angry chords all smashed together. But gradually, they break into something else. Something that's not sad or angry but hopeful, nostalgic.

Of course.

It's our song.

Past, present, future, you are

Whenever I'm far

CHAPTER 11

Wynona

Sleep's supposed to bring you clarity, or rest at the very least.

But I feel as unclear as I did yesterday, and even more tired.

Then again, at least I'm in a rainforest.

I take a slow inhale then exhale as I eye my surroundings.

Everywhere I look, there's another lush green, glistening gorgeous specimen of nature that you definitely wouldn't find back in NYC, let alone the USA. What gets me is the sheer number of them, these plants. Each tree branch seems to hold a mini-forest of its own, monsteras, orchids, and other plants I don't know the names of all coating its mossy surface together.

They're even taking over the one bench I've come across, although that doesn't stop me from sitting down on it.

Because, let's face it, as much as I'm loving the hotel's free excursion to the nearby rainforest, I'm not here for the view.

I'm here to think.

I managed to avoid Emerson this morning—unless he was avoiding me. At any rate, I can't just avoid and refuse to speak to him indefinitely.

Last night already seemed... unfair enough as it is. Emerson had a point. Why jump to conclusions, and the worst ones at that?

And wasn't it childish, talking to him through the door like that, point-blank refusing to hear him out?

Maybe. Probably.

The thing is, I wasn't in any state to hear him out, harmless truth or not.

Eyes already streaming, nose already kill-me-now red, he'd have thought I was a complete wreck.

So... better for him to think I'm a spaz instead?

I sigh.

Normally, I'd just hit up Josie and get her take, except this time, I both know it and don't want it.

Yes, I acted like a silly child. Yes, I should just go and talk to him. And... yes, I should do that right now.

Instead of hiding away in this dewy rainforest like the next course of action to take is this big mystery.

As if I haven't been jumping at every other thing Emerson's done, sure that it proved my worst-case-scenario mind right.

I change the cross of my legs, shooing away a bug that looks like a mosquito. I knew I should've worn bug spray...

My mind wanders back to an argument Josie and I had a few months back...

"Sorry for being a realist," I grumbled in reply.

Josie threw her head back and laughed. "Realist?"

"Yeah," I snapped. "I don't have my head up in the clouds, always expecting things to 'turn out for the best' and waiting for 'everything to work out'. I go by facts, by likelihoods."

Josie just looked at me like I couldn't possibly understand. "You just rename your pessimism 'realism' and then go from there."

"No," I said without pausing to even think about it. Although when I pause to think about it now, my "no" was a bit shaky.

"Yes," she said. "Reality is subjective. Confirmation bias is real. Why not believe in the best possible scenario?"

"Because it's delusional," I found myself saying. "Because it's a fast road to disappointment, to disillusionment. Then you won't be prepared."

Josie just quirked an eyebrow. She didn't have to say a word. I knew what that eyebrow was saying. Do I look like someone who's disillusioned, disappointed, and unprepared?

"Look," I said, measuring my tone. "The whole world is like me. We've run the numbers, looked at the facts. The planet is screwed, we're all screwed, and the average person is a selfish piece of shit who only cares about one-upping their peers. What's the point in moseying along like a brainless blind idiot pretending otherwise?"

Suddenly, Josie shot me one of those rare lucid looks of hers that seem to cut straight to things. "Problems aren't solved on the level of thinking they were created."

I rolled my eyes. "Thanks, Socrates."

"You can thank Einstein," she says. "Although it's some logic that I'd think you, of all people, would appreciate. In what state do you think the average person or society is in a better position to handle its problems, a terrified, negative, fearful one or a positive, go-getter one?"

I could feel her points tugging at me like a thrusting branch as I'm striding by.

"We're talking about positive, delusional people who don't accept facts," I snapped.

"No," Josie said, looking at me with a compassion that annoyed me even more. "We're talking about you, Wyn. About how you use your 'logic' and 'realism' argument to justify being a downer twenty-four, seven." She shrugged. "It doesn't bother me. As you say, I'm delusional anyway. But it must not be fun for you."

I shrugged. "It's probably not fun for most of us. But we're here and we're making the best of it. I guess that's what you do when it's the end of the world."

Josie's face went hard, her eyes far-off, sad and happy and alight. "No, when it's the end of the world, you fight it till the end, then, when there's no more denying it, you dance and smile a little, thankful that you were one of the lucky ones who got to be there at the last."

Her words had a strange poetic lilt. Josie used to be into that kind of thing until a poetry-loving Italian dumped her.

I didn't say anything because Josie's words made a kind of sense.

"And at the end of the day," she finished, "it's not practical."

"Yeah, okay," I said.

She shrugged. "It's not. It's not practical because it doesn't make you happy. Even if I'm wrong and delusional and out-of-touch, it doesn't matter, don't you get it? Because going around with your 'reality glasses' and seeing everything in the worst possible way makes you miserable. So, what's the point? What's the point of being 'realistic' if it makes you miserable?"

At the time, I rolled my eyes and stormed off and hid Josie's favorite BBQ kettle chips as retribution. Busy in the routine of working and dating and walking the dog and repeat, I never gave it much thought since.

But here it is again, clouding everything, this negativity like a vise around my life.

And yet, isn't being witty and wry and sad and sarcastic, with my dark humor and tragic tales, just being me? Isn't that how I bond with the other sad ones who see it too? Aren't they more exciting, dynamic, and mysterious, these people who carry a bit of the world's darkness in themselves?

Even Emerson. He's blond and wholesome and, at base, a good guy, but that wasn't what drew me to him. It was his little darkness which he'd shown me late one night when it was just us—the mom who never called, the dad who hardly knew who he was.

At the end of the day, it's not practical.

I switch the cross of my legs again. Two girls with Jamaican braids stride by, looking at me like they know.

Does Josie have a point?

This 'realism' of mine, is it wearing thin? Is it more trouble than it's worth? Have I really renamed 'pessimism' 'realism'?

And what, if anything, is the alternative?

I get up, starting to walk I don't know where.

What it comes down to is that I'm just putting off the inevitable, talking to Emerson and finding out the truth.

These here are just mental exertions. They won't come to anything.

And yet…

I can't go on with my life like this, jumping at shadows and seeing the worst in everything I lay eyes on.

Emerson and I will never work unless I trust him, trust myself, trust that things can maybe go well. But I don't know how.

If my pessimism is just pessimism and no good at all, I don't know what to do with it. It's all I've ever known.

My wanderings take me to the beach. I take off my black and white striped Mary Janes and chuckle at how they are so not beach shoes.

I plop down onto the sand, which molds like memory foam to my butt, and look out at the waves upon waves upon waves. I've got on my hat and sunscreen, and the sun is baking my paleness into a tan.

"What are you thinking about?"

It's him. Of course, it's him.

He sits beside me and looks where I'm looking.

I'm as surprised as he is at what comes out of my mouth. "Wondering if the world's going to end."

He manages to chuckle. "Oh, only that?"

I chuckle too. "Minor things."

And then, because if I put it off any longer I'll never say it, I tell him, "I'm sorry. About before."

I don't look at him because I don't want whatever else I say to be shaped by the curve of his smile or his frown. I want it to be mine. I want it to be real.

"I don't think it will," he says finally. "Us humans, we're too adaptive for that. We'll find a way. Whether it's in the last year or month or week we have, we'll find it."

"About before," he continues. "That was my ex. Mary. The one I told you about."

"I figured as much," I say.

The hard breakup one. Of course.

"But I didn't ask her to come," he continues. "Shit, we haven't been in contact for six months. She just showed up out of the blue.

Must've found out that I stayed on after the wedding. I'd gotten a few texts from her in the past week and a half, but I just ignored them."

"And?"

Emerson's expression doesn't reveal much. Annoyance, if anything.

"And she showed up just as I was leaving your room," he says. "Wanted to get back together. Came all the way here to tell me in person."

"And?"

"And I'm past over it."

With my heel, I'm digging a hole in the sand. Who knows why?

"Emerson," I say, careful to keep my voice steady, "if you want to get back together with her... I just want you to know that you don't owe me anything."

His laugh is incredulous, annoyed. "You think I'm here because I think I owe you something?"

I shrug.

"Seeing her in person confirmed it for me," Emerson says. "I don't feel anything for her anymore."

"Just like that?" I say softly.

It seems, again, too good to be true.

"Just like that," he says. "Hell, even when I was with her, yeah, I was crazy about her for a time, but..."

"It was never the same," I finish for him.

Our eyes find each other.

"I'd go through the motions with them," I say quietly, hardly believing I'm daring to. "But it always fell short."

"There was always something missing," Emerson says. "And that almost made it worse when she dumped me. Since I never thought she'd be the one to do it."

"But it's been so long that you almost forget," I continue half-consciously.

"What it's like," he says, hands finding mine.

And this time, when our eyes find each other, there's not the slightest doubt that we're thinking the same thing.

"So now?" I say.

He shrugs. "She said she'd booked a night here. I assume that she's gone by now. Although she did try sneaking into my room to surprise me."

He says it too nonchalantly. I glance his way.

"All right, she was naked," he admits, scowling. "But I sent her away without touching her, I swear."

"I believe you," I say, giggling a little. I'm so surprised at how readily the belief comes. "But you weren't tempted even a bit?"

"No," he says, scowling. "Fucking weird is what it is."

"You like me," I sing-song. "You really like me."

"Don't let it go to your head," he growls, then exhales. "All right, I like you."

We sit there comfortably as all the tension I hadn't even realized I was holding in my neck and shoulders eases away.

"I don't know if I'm ready for this," I say.

"Neither do I," he says.

"I wanted to go slow, but… slow doesn't exist for me when I'm with you," I say.

I can hear him shift to look at me. "And you think it does for me?"

"I don't know how to trust you again," I say. "All that you told me... I trust that you were telling the truth and I trust you to an extent, but after what happened... I just keep feeling like things will go wrong again."

Emerson lets my words sit long enough for me to say something else. A lot of something elses.

We let the afternoon sea breeze take the words and throw them away.

A seagull laughs somewhere. An unseen child wails. And who's listening to Moby right now, and here, of all places?

"They might," he says when he finally says what he's been thinking. "As for trusting me fully, I don't know if you should."

I can't help it. I look at him.

He makes torture look handsome, the way his sculpted face is a study of pain.

"I'm never not going to look out for you, Wynona," he says.

And he takes my hands.

And he looks at me.

"I'm always going to do what I think is best for you," he says. "Even if it means I can't be with you."

I look at him.

And I rip my hands free.

"What kind of answer is that?" A laugh, a cry falls out of me. "What the hell, Emerson?"

"I was holding you back. It needed to end."

"And now? What if it happens again?"

"I won't let it happen again."

"You can't control everything."

"No," he says, louder now, like a verbal shaking of a fist. "I can't. But I can make damn sure that we aren't apart like that again. That I don't let you suffer like that again."

His hand seeks mine. I let it keep on seeking. "But how can you be sure…"

"I can't." His voice is ragged. "I don't know anything for sure except that I want to try. Right now, that's enough for me."

His hand catches mine. Mine wasn't really trying to evade it, not hard, anyway.

"Wynona?" he says as if my hand in his isn't an answer already.

"It's enough for me," I say finally.

And then our eyes are meeting again, and I don't think I've ever seen a blue like his before. The kind of blue you could throw half a dozen adjectives at and not get close.

When we kiss, I know.

I'm not afraid anymore.

He pulls away smiling, although I can see it's hard for him. "I've got a surprise for you."

CHAPTER 12

Emerson

"A surprise?" she says.

Her tone suggests an exotic dish that could be slimy octopus arms or her favorite—grilled lemon shrimp.

Good thing I know my girl well.

Inwardly, I wince.

'My girl'. Fucking Christ, you're losing it, Emerson.

"C'mon," I say, rising. "Let me show you. You're going to love it."

It feels damn good walking down the sunny beach with her hand in mine.

She's a prize, my Wynona.

Her every comment is funny or interesting or both.

She's telling me about her trip to the rainforest this afternoon, and I'm only half-listening because I'm so excited to see what she'll think of it. What I have to show her.

When we stop in front of it, she doesn't understand.

"If this is a party..." she says.

"What?" I joke. "You don't go to parties now?"

"No," she says. "But if that's your idea of a surprise..."

"They are called surprise parties for a reason," I quip, although I'm already shaking my head. "It's not that."

"Hmm." She taps her lip. "You got them to give us a private boat ride?"

"Guess again," I tell her.

"I'm all out of guesses," she says. "Tell me!"

"It's ours," I say nonchalantly, striding onto the boat.

Wynona stands there, staring at me. "Ours?"

"Okay," I amend. "It's mine, but yeah. I bought a boat. Crazy, yeah?"

She laughs, grins, then nods. "Yeah."

"Too crazy for you to even consider coming on?"

Next second, she's taken my hand and stepped onto the boat. "Not that crazy. Although I should ask, do you even know how to work this thing?"

"Nolan and I went boating in a friend's that was similar before the wedding," I say. "Plus, Dad would always have us drive him around in his motorboat when we went to his Florida condo."

"All I ask is that you don't kill us," Wynona says primly.

I just smirk. "I can't make any promises."

"Jerk."

"Winnie."

"Don't you dare call me that. You know I hated it when Josie used to!"

I catch her in my arms, and then we're laughing and kissing and laughing at how awkward laughing makes our kissing.

"You," Wynona says, pausing to press a purple-nailed finger into my chest.

She looks delighted and disgruntled and wildly beautiful.

I want to kiss that purple lipstick off her. I want to kiss her all over this boat.

She extricates herself, though, smiling shyly. "Did you show me this boat to use it or to kiss me on it?"

"Why not both?" I say, though she has a point. "Now, let's see what this baby can do."

Minutes later, we're off the coast, in the deep blue sea, zooming along at top speed.

Wynona's sitting at the prow on the leather seat, beaming as we zip along.

I'd have bought this boat just for that, the sight of just how happy she is right now.

"What are you going to do?" she asks.

"Huh?"

"With the boat." A smile, like it's obvious. "When you leave, silly."

I smile too. "Haven't decided yet." I shrug. "Maybe resell it before I leave. No concerts on the immediate horizon, so…"

Wynona nods in understanding.

"Though I do have savings," I tell her so she doesn't think I'm completely hard up.

A judicious nod, an extravagant eye flutter, a falsetto voice, and Wynona declares, "Glad you're not after me for my money."

"Hell no." Making a face, I cut the power, reaching for her. "I'm after you for your ass."

"You ass!" she declares, laughing and smacking me.

I take her in my arms and spin her around, my hands settling on her firm, so-good ass. "But it's such a nice ass."

Our lips meet, although she peels away to declare, "You're a complete perv."

"Don't shoot the messenger." I kiss back.

Fuck yeah, she feels good in my arms.

A kind of rightness that defies words. Logic, even.

How our bodies move together... shit.

I kiss her into the steering wheel, kiss off her loose-fitting boho top and teal cherry-print bathing suit top.

"But Emerson." She couples her protest with a half-hearted attempt to extricate herself.

I gesture at the 360 degrees of blue. "There's no one for miles."

She cranes her neck around, then, apparently satisfied as her lips reach for mine, says, "If anyone sees, I'll kill you."

"A risk I'm willing to take," I say, and then my lips are claiming hers again.

With her on my slouched lap, I get a nice close-up of those beautiful pert tits, the creamy white skin of her breast, the jutting pink of her nipple just begging to be caressed.

Naturally, I oblige.

So soft, so firm... they fit so nicely into each of my palms.

Her head droops back, spilling her jet-black hair behind her, and a long, low moan rolls out of her elegant throat. I tip her chin back toward me and straighten myself upright so my lips can have hers some more.

'Kissing' isn't the right word. Not for what happens when our lips find each other. Or how our tongues join in, sometimes just punctuation, sometimes leading, sometimes nothing at all.

How our bodies join in, stroking and feeling and touching and exploring and finding.

Her nipples are hard between my fingers. Her hand strokes my hardness harder.

She smells damn good, tastes even better.

Her shorts come off easily, showcasing a matching bright teal bathing suit bottom with vibrant red cherries depicted on it. Although I only spare them a passing glance. It's her ass I can't seem to draw my hands away from.

"An amazing ass," I murmur.

She throws her head back and laughs, the big, contagious kind that you can't help but be swept up in.

I caress it and smack it and enjoy how she croons. I jiggle it and hold it, and then my hands slide forward, meeting at the front of her cherry bikini bottoms, pressing into the wetness that isn't from swimming.

"Emerson," she murmurs.

"Wynona," I growl.

My fingers stroke all around, enjoying how she squirms. And then, I dip one finger in.

"Emerson," she groans, louder now.

I vibrate it, dipping it in further.

"Emerson," she moans even louder.

I dip both fingers in, stroking and fingering her.

Goddamn, she's crazy-wet. And turned on.

I love seeing her like this.

So into it.

I finger her until she's sunk into me, shaking.

Then, in one smooth motion, I take off my swim trunks.

She takes one look at my hard-as-fuck cock, and she says, "Please."

She doesn't have to ask me twice.

I lift her up and onto me, where I'm sitting on the front seat. Seconds later, she's riding me like a pro.

Those pretty pert tits jiggle as she grinds her hips back and forth. She'll be deep in an amazing rhythm, bobbing up and down on my dick when suddenly, she'll switch the angle up, and new shots of pleasure go through me.

She comes all at once, and then I flip her around so she's on the chair and I'm drilling her fast and hard. We ride her orgasm higher as she cries out, "Yes!!!" and then I'm coming too.

Somehow, we end up on the floor of the boat, her in my arms, watching the clouds drag past.

One looks like a three-legged poodle, another a man with a lasso.

"That was good," I say.

Since I can't think of anything else to say.

She rolls on her side to eye me. "Oh, yeah?"

"Yeah."

"Banging me on a boat?"

"Now that you mention it… it does have a nice ring."

She snorts. "Great."

My hand idles in her glossy black strands. "Things are easier like that."

Her gaze manages to be sardonic yet guarded. "You mean when we're not talking?"

I frown. "You really like conflict, don't you?"

She considers that. "It does have a way of bringing things out in the open."

"True," I admit.

I roll on my side to look at her.

It doesn't seem wise, noticing how beautiful she looks right now. That ivory skin with its subtle curves, the bare-lipped half-smile like she's got a good secret.

Something tightens in me, and I sit up.

"Emerson?" she says.

"Just thinking," I say.

Her silence is a question in itself, an opening. But I get up and go start up the motor.

The breeze hits all of me, and I remember.

Shit.

I pull on my clothes, then sit down, steering us to where we're headed.

Wynona's voice is a quiet accusation. "That's it?"

"What's it?"

"You just drive us out somewhere secluded so we can screw on your boat, then it's time to go back?"

I turn to look at her. "No."

Her scowl is unconvinced. "Really."

"Really," I say. "That was part one."

"And you were planning on telling me..."

"Didn't think of it," I say, turning back to the steering wheel.

If I'm going to get us there, I'm going to have to pay attention.

I can't say why this mood has come over me. I don't want to think about it.

It'd bring me back to those first weeks without her, all those years back.

When it dawned on me.

Just what I'd done.

The uselessness that followed that phone call. The months of fighting with myself. Regret like a noose I hanged myself on each and every morning.

By the time I got better enough to check up on her... she was better too.

Better enough that I knew I couldn't, no matter how much I wanted to, get back together.

The months after that were the worst. I could hardly play piano, could hardly sleep.

Every girl seemed glaringly off with how much she wasn't her.

Everyone was sympathetic at first, kept saying things about time.

Time just laughed and gave me the finger.

Time just reached into my body and gave my heart a wrench every time I thought about her.

And back then, I swore—never again. Never a-fucking-gain.

And now...

No.

I give my head a determined shake.

Better not to think about it.

I breathe in the sea air wet with spray, stretch my hot palms on the cool wood of the steering wheel, and steady my stance on the buzzing boat floor. I pick out the landmarks that I marked in my mental map when I looked up the route earlier today.

There's the rocky shoreline of the small island. There's the far-off pale purple-green peak of Mount Maggie.

"Nearly there," I tell Wynona.

When we pull up on shore, I drop the anchor then help her out of the boat. We don't have far to go to reach the mouth of the cave.

It's a rocky hill that looks out of place. Like it has no business being here.

It took me an hour of random online searching of forums before I stumbled upon it.

It looks even bigger than I expected.

One step inside, and I'm stopping, peering further in. The beam of my flashlight reveals an endless-seeming cavern with stalactites like fangs hanging from the ceiling.

"This is cool," Wynona admits as I take her hand and we venture further in.

"Not still mad at me?" I tease her.

"Oh, I am," she says simply.

We pick our way across the slick, uneven stone floor. It smells dank in here.

A curse, then Wynona abruptly jerks down on my arm. I just manage to catch her before she wipes out on the ground.

"Damn it, my stupid flip-flops," she says, lifting a broken blue plastic one miserably.

"Not the best for cave exploring," I say.

She shoots me a withering glare. "Well, if I'd been warned…"

I crouch down, then gesture her forward, onto my back. "Lucky for you, you have a superior method of transportation."

Wynona doesn't move. "Emerson, I don't know."

I turn to scowl at her. "Think I can't handle it? Try me."

She shrugs. "If you fall and kill us, it's your funeral."

I just smile. "Nah. It's both our funerals."

She rolls her eyes. "Great, that makes me feel all warm and fuzzy."

She comes up and clambers on my back, then we venture in further until the entrance is a speck far behind us.

"How far are we going?" Wynona asks.

"This far enough?" I ask her.

"Five minutes ago was," she says, getting off and sitting down. "But this will do."

"Good," I say.

"Good," she says.

The cave makes our voices echo.

There's no more slickness here. Just us and rock.

"Sorry about before," I find myself saying.

Wynona doesn't say anything.

"This is all new to me," I admit.

"And it isn't to me?" she asks. "You broke my heart, Emerson. I hated you for a very long time."

"Maybe you were right to."

"That's it?"

"No. Just... that's what made it harder for me. That I had chosen to do this. To end things with you."

"You're not going to get any sympathy from me."

"I don't expect any."

A sigh. "I'm sorry. I keep meaning to be less bitchy, and then I go and be bitchy again."

"It's all right," I tell her. "I'm sorry too."

She lets the silence sit. It's almost nice, her easing into my arms.

Only, there's one thing that's missing right now.

"Kiss me," I say.

"You first," she says.

I kiss her and then she snuggles into me further, and I hold her.

Of course I want her. Of course I want to fuck her right here, right now.

I know how hot her lithe body is. I know how it moves with mine.

But this moment—right here, right now—it's enough.

Just as it is.

Right here. Right now.

**

Back at the hotel, I walk Wynona to her door. We kiss goodnight.

By the time I think to check my phone messages back in my room, it's almost midnight. One is a spam call, but the last one makes me sit down on my bed and listen to it.

And another time. And another time.

And then I lie on my bed staring at nothing.

CHAPTER 13

Wynona

"You free tonight?" Emerson asks when he calls me at noon.

The morning was waking up so late it felt luxurious. I had a quick catch-up French toast breakfast with Josie in person and Mom over Skype—apparently, the dogs have stopped knocking over her plants—a nice long shower, and coming up with and dismissing the idea of calling up Emerson several times.

I almost smile "Maybe."

"Fine," Emerson says, suddenly short. "If you don't want the VIP suite I booked—"

"Whoa," I say. "What's your problem?"

"You're playing games again."

I sigh, then chuckle a little self-consciously. "Maybe I should be asking what my problem is."

"That's obvious," Emerson says, back to good-humored confidence. "You're not in the VIP suite I booked us yet."

I smile. "A mistake you're about to rectify, by the sound of it?"

"I'll come get you in two hours," he says.

Those two hours I spend sketching out a colorful new logo for my tattoo business—the old one is very out-of-date—and then stalking Emerson on Google. There's not much to find, other than a few very handsome photos, so I actually get around to hanging up my clothes.

By the time he shows up, I've had on my black velvet skater skirt and deep blue velvet tee for about an hour, my black cat-eye makeup done for a half-hour.

"You look great," he says.

It almost seems repetitive, his saying it, with the way his eyes are resting on me already.

"You too," I say.

My own gaze lingers on him, on his powerful shoulders in the deep purple dress shirt he's wearing and on his black tailored pants.

I feel underdressed, even though Josie agreed my outfit was 'fancy enough'.

It's a quick walk down the hallway, rounding a corner, and then another, then, opening the door until…

"Well, damn," is the first thing I say when I set foot into the VIP suite.

It's like walking into a work of art, with every last detail customized to please. Floors, walls, and ceiling are a creamy rose marble twined with gold while the muted teal and gold bedspread and gold-leaf furniture are nothing short of gorgeous. Even the smell seems to match, a subtle, classy mix of vanilla and roses.

Emerson indicates a balcony visible through the glass doors. "That's what convinced me this would be worth it."

I venture further into the room, although my gaze is stuck on the balcony overlooking the rainforest with two hammocks swaying gently side to side, as if in wait.

I pause, another scent catching my attention, and whirl around to see a glass and gold table in the corner set with golden cutlery and two plates of roasted salmon and grilled vegetables.

Emerson rubs at his chin with a pleased nod. "So that was why they wanted to know the exact time I planned on arriving."

We sit down and eat. Every bite is delicious, with an unusual mix of spices and flavors I can't put my finger on. The texture, the give of the salmon under my teeth—it's all perfect.

And then, of course, there's the handsome man across from me with his own sort of perfection.

I'm just chewing my last roasted zucchini when Emerson's phone goes off.

"Hey, Landon," he says, picking it up. "Can't really talk right now."

"It's fine," I tell him, but he shakes his head.

"Can't talk now," he repeats more firmly. "Yeah, having dinner with Wynona right now, actually. Yeah, you, too."

He hangs up with a chuckle. "He was worried about me. But he doesn't need to be. Not with the great company I have."

"Flattery will get you everywhere," I quip as he moves a forkful of sautéed cauliflower to my lips.

As I bite into it, our gazes meet.

Heat flushes between my legs.

Jesus.

Only Emerson could make me feel sexy while eating a freaking piece of cauliflower, of all things.

Our gazes hold as I chew it, then swallow. Then, our lips land together.

A twist of lips, teeth, and tongue. He grabs the back of my head and holds it there, holds us there.

He tastes like the meal we just ate and kisses like I'm dessert.

"God, you're fucking hot," he breathes between kisses.

Both his hands go on either side of my face as he kisses me. He kisses me wildly and he kisses me hard.

When we pull away again, we're out of breath.

He's wearing a dark musky cologne that's got my thoughts jumbled all over each other.

Like how I've never had a man look at me with the kind of want Emerson does. The kind of intensity that doesn't seem safe—and yet makes any other attraction seem paltry in comparison.

"Wynona," he says, scowling suddenly.

He closes his eyes and exhales. "The cake will get cold."

I have to laugh. "That's what you're thinking about right now?"

He shrugs and gives his head an I'm-annoyed-yet-pleased roll. "Only the best for my girl."

I quirk an eyebrow. "Oh, is that what I am, now?"

He gives the smile nod that you give to the slow child who finally grasped 1 + 1 = 2. "Glad you're finally catching on."

I snort. "Because you've been so upfront about everything."

"I've tried to be."

"Wonderful."

"Great."

Our eyes do a battle of their own, while he uses his fork to cut a piece of the cake. He lifts it to my mouth. Eyes still on him, I bite down.

Blueberry-chocolate richness awakens my taste buds.

"Good?" he asks.

"Why not have a taste?" I offer him.

Next thing I know, our lips are locked again.

"You," he growls, the flats of his palms pressing down my body like they can't help themselves, "aren't making this easy on me, are you?"

I pull away, taking his lip with me part of the way. "Want me to stop?"

My voice is all innocence, but my smirk is pure devilry.

Emerson's response is to grab me and set me on his lap. "That's better."

Our lips find each other's again.

Emerson kisses with a hunger, a power, a leading that I have no choice but to follow. The twining and untwining of our lips and our tongues is a flow that's always leading further, seeking more.

The slightest of teeth on my lips, while his hands trace the curve of my rib cage to my waist to my hips, almost puts me on the edge.

Have I ever been this horny when clothed?

Our kiss moves us off the chair and away from the table, all the way to the wall. He presses me into it. I straddle him and our pelvises rub together.

Fuck, I can feel how hard he is through his pants, even with four layers separating us.

Another kiss and my dress is riding up. Another, and he's taking off his pants.

Only two layers now.

He kisses me onto the bed, covering my body with his. He pulls off his briefs as I pull off my soaked panties.

No layers now.

Pussy and cock grind together until he's about to slip inside me and...

"No." I groan, my pussy straining for him.

That jerk, he teased my opening, only going in partially.

"Yeah?" Emerson grunts, twisting his lips on mine.

"Yeah," I pull away to say.

Another grinding together, and he—oh, fuck yes!—finally dips into me, but oh, fuck no, he's pulling out as my pussy trembles with pleasured frustration.

"Say please," Emerson growls.

"Fuck you," I say.

He rubs his cock across my opening.

I'm so flushed and horny I can't think straight.

"Please," I groan, and then, finally, finally, he's inside me, piercing me deeply.

A wail rolls out of my throat. Trembling takes over my body.

It feels. So. Goddamn. Good.

I'm so filled. So full.

Emerson grunts with pleasure, then repeats the thrust, plunging deep inside me.

Deep… and deeper. And deeper.

There are no words. Only sensations. Only perfection heaped on perfection.

Our bodies were made for each other.

And his is showing mine just what it needs.

It's only another minute before I'm coming, although Emerson isn't done yet. Not nearly.

He moves me so I'm on my side and then starts plowing me again.

It feels fucking amazing.

Soon, I'm coming again, and his face is gritted with happy exertion.

Finally, he props my legs onto his chest, then, together, we come, crying out.

Afterward, in bed, we finish the rest of the dessert.

I'm so warm, so cozy, so happy. Emerson's strong arms are around me, chocolatey-blueberry goodness in my mouth.

Afterward, we lie there.

"This time is going to be different," Emerson says quietly when he does finally speak.

My heart leaps.

Because maybe it was just one instance, but still, Emerson told his brother about me, about us… so that's something.

Not nearly enough to prove that he meant what he said, or even to set us sure on the right path. Not yet, anyway. But it's something.

I can feel myself dozing off, but I force myself upright. "Want to check out the balcony? If we stay here, I'm definitely passing out."

Emerson's response is to rise and, with no warning, pick me up.

"Emerson!" I squeal.

His smirk is the definition of unrepentant. "If I let you go, then you'd put on clothes."

I giggle as he carries me to the glass door, then out onto the balcony. "And I suppose what I want doesn't make any difference?"

"Not in the slightest."

Emerson places me carefully in a hammock, then gets into the one next to me. At first, it seems to bend my body at a whole bunch of odd angles, forcing its will on me. But then I relax and let go, and

I find the hammock forming itself to me as it gently rocks me back and forth.

With the angle I'm at, I have a gorgeous view of the darkening greens of the rainforest and the final splash of orange-yellow on the horizon.

What is it about being around Emerson that makes me hyper-aware to my surroundings at the most unexpected times? It's like finally finding glasses with the right prescription.

Is it love?

Or is it just a relaxation, a loosening?

Because when I think about it, my fear of being alone, of being one of those sad, lonely old women you feel sorry for, for as long as I've been single, it's been there, lurking, like the black dog Churchill spoke of.

Of course, in being single, there's the freedom and the possibility as wide as the sky and as numerous as the cute guys I see every day, but I've never quite reached the state of 'single bliss' all the magazines, self-help books, and the odd well-meaning acquaintance always promoted. Even months into it, while there was something fun and sassy about going to movies or restaurants alone, or going home instead of hooking up, I still couldn't be quite at ease with the thought that this is all it is and ever will be.

Maybe, once I stop worrying so much about the things I have so little control over, I can notice how very beautiful this world is.

Like sunsets aren't just nice screensavers or good photos. They're vibrant, real things.

"I'm glad I chose this," Emerson says.

"Me too," I agree.

"I knew it'd suit you," he continues, reaching over to squeeze my hand. "The other room had an infinity pool, but I know how you like your hammocks."

I chuckle and shoot him a surprised glance. "That one time I was on the hunt for one in my apartment, you remembered?"

He shrugs. "The infinity pool was more Insta-worthy, but I know that's not your style."

My smile is rueful. "You never know, I could've changed."

Emerson shoots me an appraising sidelong glance. "Do you even have Instagram, Wynona?"

"My business does," I admit. "Business necessity. But me, myself? Nah. I used to, though."

"Yeah?"

"Yeah. I spent a bunch of time looking at pretty people with pretty lives and a bit of time wondering why mine wasn't the same. It's insidious, that, a kind of unfocused jealousy. I deleted it after a few months."

Emerson nods, squeezing my hand absently. "It gets to the point where you do things to have something to show and tell other people about, not for the enjoyment of doing them."

I nod too. "I heard a quote once, about pictures you take on vacation, that I've never forgotten. That years later, it ends up that practically the only things you remember about those trips and times are the pictures. Your memory gets lazy, relies on them like the only benchmarks it has."

Emerson's quiet for a good long while.

Further off, monkeys hoot and birds caw, but here, it's quiet.

When Emerson finally speaks, he says, "I guess now isn't the time to say we should take a picture together."

I chuckle. "Is it for a benchmark for your memory, or to brag on Instagram?"

His chuckle changes into a grin. "Neither. Something for me to look at and enjoy."

"All right," I say, "but I'm holding the phone. You men wouldn't know a good angle if it hit you in the face."

Emerson just laughs.

So, I hold his phone and take the photos, one, two... a bunch more.

After, we look at the photos, although I keep on holding his phone and looking at it even after Emerson's gone back to his own hammock.

Jesus, I haven't looked this happy since...

Forget it.

"I was thinking," Emerson says at the same time I hand him back his phone.

I pause, waiting for the rest of his sentence.

It never comes.

"What were you thinking?" I finally ask, eyeing the final slivers of the sunset.

"Forget it," Emerson says.

"All right," I say.

I could argue with him. I could force him and grumble at him until he tells me.

But I'm tired of forcing things, tired of assuming that if I don't, they won't go my way.

I'm tired of assuming there's something important in Emerson's every unsaid thought or look. It's too tiring.

Emerson's done enough for me these past few days—the dinner, this VIP suite, and taking me out on his boat.

It's enough. It has to be enough.

It's a slippery slope, looking outside for everything you need. Looking for proof that someone cares, proof that your weakest, worst thoughts are wrong.

What Josie said about confirmation bias... that is a thing. The placebo effect, whatever you want to call it. Seeing what you expect to see.

I've been guilty of it a fair bit, lately. But I don't want to be, not now.

So, I take Emerson's hand and I bring it to my lips. I let the hammocks sway me and my heartbeat slower.

It could be ten minutes we've been here, side by hammock side, or it could be over an hour. Checking the time would only ruin it, this pause we're in.

"Wynona," Emerson says suddenly, his voice sounding odd in the quiet. "What would you say to staying longer?"

"Longer?"

"Longer," he says. "It's almost time to go back. I don't want to."

"But my business..." I say, trailing off.

"You don't have to decide right now," he says, annoyed. "It was just a thought."

"And our plane tickets?"

"They were fine to reschedule a week later," he says casually. "Dad had an old friend at the airline's head office and I called him up."

I always thought it was weird, people getting speechless when something intense happens. Couldn't they just blurt out something, no matter how stupid?

But right now, I am. Literally. Speechless.

Emerson wants to stay longer? Even called to confirm it was possible?

And what about me? What do I want?

A low sigh escapes my lips. It's not about what I want to do. It's about what I should do.

My business, my dogs… I can't keep on pretending that I don't have a real life waiting for me back home, no matter how much of an amazing time I'm having with Emerson.

"When we go home—" I begin tentatively.

"I want to keep seeing you," Emerson cuts in abruptly.

I look at him, at his hard eyes like a challenge, his tense mouth a statement.

"Okay," I say.

He chuckles. "Okay."

"So, we're allowed to go home?" I say.

"I guess," he says. "Think about it, though. Another week or half-week here could be nice."

"It could," I admit. "It is slow season for tattoos, and if I gave my customers ten percent off for the wait, I could maybe get away with it…"

"But I haven't decided yet," I finish, catching his excited look.

He shrugs, turning away. "We've got time."

I don't say the next part, I like it when you say 'we'.

Next time I wake up, I'm in bed, in Emerson's arms. He's asleep.

The next time I wake up, I'm in bed. But Emerson is gone.

CHAPTER 14

Emerson

"What do you think?" I ask Jeremy when we meet up at the bar.

Even though Wynona looked to be asleep, this is one conversation I don't want her overhearing. And it's been a while since I touched based with Jeremy. Not that I worried. Even when we were kids, he would disappear for days and reappear days later with seemingly no explanation.

This time, his red Mohawk looks pricklier than usual, but he otherwise seems his normal lanky, long-faced self.

"It's a great opportunity," he admits. "They don't come around often."

"Almost never," I agree grimly, thinking back to the call.

Who knew that the aloe vera guy Nolan introduced me to, Yolan, would actually come through with the offer to go on tour? The money is good, and the potential coverage is good. Only the timing is bad.

"But going on tour for six months..." I say, thinking out loud. "And Wynona..."

"A tough decision," Jeremy says with an understanding nod. "And one I can't make for you."

"I've made up my mind, anyway," I tell him. "I have to give this a proper go this time."

"Have you told her?" Jeremy asks. "About the offer to go on tour?"

"No," I admit. "I don't want to complicate this further. She doesn't need to know."

"You should tell her," Jeremy says.

A twinge of annoyance goes through me at my friend voicing what I'd felt instinctively already.

He's always had a sense about him, Jeremy has. Half a year back, when I was losing my shit and drinking way too much, he was the first one to tell me to cut it out.

Things might've been easier if I'd listened.

"This is my decision to make," I argue.

"One that affects her," he says smoothly. "Who knows? You said it yourself that she's different now."

"Damn it, Jeremy," I find myself growling. "I'm not about to make the very same mistake that broke us up last time."

"She couldn't come with you?"

"We've barely started seeing each other. It's been less than a week," I say. "And back in New York, she's got a thriving business, two dogs, and a life. I couldn't ask her to leave that behind for half a year for me."

"Makes sense," Jeremy says, swigging down the last of his beer.

He dips his head to the dance floor, where two wasted girls are grinding on each other while eyeing us pointedly. "Care to join?"

"You're joking," I say.

Jeremy sighs heavily. "Yep, you're whipped."

"Dude."

He shrugs. "Those girls are model-hot. The fact that you barely noticed means it's the real thing. You poor, poor guy."

"Yeah, yeah," I say, smiling ruefully as I rise. "I'll leave you to it?"

Jeremy grooves his way onto the dance floor with a wave flung behind him. "Good luck!"

Back in our VIP room, Wynona's half-upright on the bed, her black hair a bit ruffled and her blue eyes sleepy with accusation. "I didn't know where you went."

"Sorry," I say, forcing a smile. "I didn't want to wake you. I was in the bar talking to Jeremy, catching up."

Her blue eyes rest on me with a shade of uncertainty, but then she smiles too. "Come back to bed."

It's one of the best mornings I've had, just lazing around in bed with her. We make love and cuddle and then do it all over again. We have breakfast and make love again. We shower together. We watch some funny Spanish show on the TV.

By the time we get out of bed, we realize, in shock, that it's dinner time. We have a quick dinner at the buffet, a quickie back in my room, a shower, and then we check out the hotel club we'd been meaning to visit.

At eleven PM, the place is hopping. Its metallic purple floors and walls pulse with people dancing to spicy Latin music. I buy us some drinks, down mine fast, then nod to the dance floor. "What do you say?"

All she has to do is smile for me to know that tonight is going to be a very good night. Wynona downs her drink too, and we head for the dance floor.

The last time I saw Wynona's hips move like that, the night of the wedding, I was filled with a hopeless vague longing. And now... I hook my arm around her waist and move her to me. Our bodies dance together to the beat. Her ass is already driving my cock hard and furiously.

Back and forth, back and forth. I get us more drinks, and we dance some more. Until I can't take it anymore and kiss her full on the mouth.

She kisses me back ferociously.

Our kiss takes us back to our room, but suddenly, she stops, looking at me hard. "Emerson, I need to know."

I stare at her uncomprehendingly.

"You're not telling me something," she says. "You've been distant all day. I've tried to just let it go, but…"

"Then let it go," I growl.

I'm not ready to tell her. Not now.

"Fuck you," she hisses.

I cover her mouth with mine. "Maybe."

Our bodies make sense of what our minds can't. I fuck her hard and rough, and she gives as good as she takes.

Afterward, as we lie exhausted in bed, I wonder, When will I tell her?

CHAPTER 15

Wynona

When will he tell me?

Whatever Emerson is keeping from me, when will he tell me?

I roll over to look at him. But he isn't there.

Outside the door, I hear voices. That's two times now that I've woken up to his being on the phone.

What's going on?

I head over there to say something, but then I hear Emerson say, "I'm sorry, but my decision is final. I won't be going on the tour."

Then, he opens the door. "Whoa. Hi."

"Hi," I say.

We look at each other.

"You talking to your secret admirer again?" I tease.

He frowns. "No."

"Okay." I turn around.

No way am I going to stick around sulking here, not when Emerson is clearly hiding something from me.

"Wynona," he says.

"What?" I ask, fists balling. Don't cry—don't you dare cry. "You said this time would be different. But you're already keeping things from me."

"It's not important," he says.

"Then why not tell me?" I force myself to exhale. "I'm trying not to be a spaz, Emerson, but with how you've been distant lately, and now this—"

"It was just an offer to go on tour," he says. "That I turned down. Not important."

His face has a wooden determination to it.

"An offer to go on tour with your music?" I ask.

"What else?"

"That doesn't sound not important to me," I argue.

"Listen, Wyn," he says, exasperated already. "We can argue about this. Is that what you want?"

"No," I snap. "I just want to know the truth. What's going on? When did you get this offer?"

"A few days ago." Emerson shrugs. "But I'm not interested. It's fine."

"Not interested in a tour that could further your career?"

He looks me straight in the eyes. "I'm not about to imperil things like last time."

"And you didn't think I should have a say in it?"

"Things are complicated enough already."

I turn away, talking to the wall. "I think you should go on the tour."

"So you don't even want to try, then? Try and make this work? Try and stay another week?"

"I won't have you making that kind of sacrifice for me," I say, rounding to look at him beseechingly. "Don't you see, Emerson? You'd end up resenting me. I wouldn't want you to miss out."

"I wouldn't be."

I sit down on the bed, getting dressed in a hurry.

"Where are you going?" he says.

"To my room. To think."

Next thing I know, I'm walking down the hallway, breathing hard.

It's odd. I feel shit about the situation, obviously. But I almost feel... sick?

I lurch into my bathroom just in time, vomiting into the toilet.

Afterward, I feel glorious, like I've been freaking exorcised. As much as I love the odd spa day with Josie and Sierra, I've never had one—no matter how many deep-tissue, hot-stone massages and mani-pedis we've gotten—that made me feel anywhere near as good as a nice vomit.

But still, I'm not one to just upchuck for no particular reason. There's always a reason.

I gaze at the unappetizing contents of the toilet in confusion. As if it's evidence that could explain a thing or two to me.

Because really, I don't have the foggiest idea what it's doing there.

I didn't drink that much last night.

I'm not crazy-nervous or distraught.

Anyway, I don't vomit because I'm nervous or distraught.

I flush it down so I don't have to look at it anymore, then go to lie down.

Maybe it's the stress of getting back together with Emerson? AKA the ex.

As I lie on my back and follow the decorative root-like line formations on my ceiling with my gaze, I try thinking it over.

As much as you can think over what-to-do-when-the-wrong-thing-is-the-thing-I-want-and-he's-choosing-that.

But wrong choice or not, it does sound like Emerson has made up his mind about it.

Just an offer to go on tour. Not important…

But of course it is. Music is Emerson's calling, his dream, his life.

A warm flutter goes through me. And he's willing to give it all up for you.

Which doesn't mean I should let him.

The last thing I want is for him to throw away a good opportunity on account of me.

I lean back and do a bit of air bicycling, hoping the added endorphins might kick some hyper-thinking into action.

No dice, though.

Finally, I roll onto my stomach, heave myself out of bed, and head to Josie's room to relay the situation to her.

"Aren't you a saint," she says, crunchily, once I've given her the CliffsNotes version.

She's mid-bag through some crunchy Cheetos, her favorite. She never would share those, even when she got a family-size bag and was supposedly trying to lose weight.

"It's mostly just self-preservation," I say with a self-conscious half-chuckle. "If he gives up that tour and later ends up resenting me… that would be complete shit."

"That would," Josie agrees. "But he is an adult. And he already made his decision."

"That's what I was thinking," I agree. "But still, it is a big deal."

"He sounds like he's really serious about you," Josie says thoughtfully.

"Don't remind me." My tone is hesitantly rueful. "Part of me wonders if it's this island or magic or something."

Josie rolls her eye mid-crunch. "Please. That man has been crazy about you since day one."

"Yeah, yeah, so crazy about me that he dumped me."

"For your own good, need I remind you?"

"No," I admit. "You're probably right. I'm being stupid. My business can wait. And can you believe Mom and the dogs... ?"

"No poops inside for three days," Josie says proudly. "It's a milestone."

I chuckle. "Guess she's a pro. All right, I'm going to go give him the news."

"Which is?"

"Nosy prier," I grumble.

"Stubborn denier," she sing-songs back.

"That I'll do it," I say, my smile spreading as I say it out loud. I feel like doing cartwheels that would result in an injury, jumping up and down like a fool. At the very least, some victorious fist-pumping. "I'll stay."

"That's my girl," Josie says with a nod and a final orange-crumbed grin. "Now shoo."

"You will?" Emerson says a few minutes later when I tell him, still standing in his doorway and practically bouncing on my toes. "You're sure?"

I laugh. "No. Are you?"

He laughs, then hugs me. "Hell no. But—hell, we're actually doing this!"

He picks me up and spins me around. I get a big whiff of him—his clean, woodsy, manly musk.

Our kiss tastes like victory.

I've never had a kiss be victorious, but I guess this is it. I guess this is what it's like when you want the same thing and you get it. When the triumphant music in your head plays just the same tune. Or at least an accompanying harmony.

If I had to describe what music is playing here as he holds me tight in his strong, warm arms, it would be jazz. Something with a sharp, staccato tempo, all upward chords and sweeps, and yet slow and rhythmic and inescapable like the mournful tuba in the background. Not taking the foreground, not in the least, and yet there all the same.

The little voice in the back of my head, with the conviction of a tried-and-true saying, If it feels too good to be true, it probably is.

And here's the thing. I've learned how to make killer tattoos—the kind of designs other people post on Pinterest or Instagram and stamp their lying names on. I've learned how to run a business and balance the rent and the tools and the marketing and everything else to get a good profit. I've learned how to not give up when the seventeenth guy I date turns out to be Dud #17.

But I haven't learned how to prove that little voice in the back of my head wrong.

Not yet.

CHAPTER 16

Emerson

Calling up airlines and getting bounced around by operators, some foreign and unintelligible, some local and bored, some a varying combination of the two, before arguing with a supervisor and being transferred to a higher supervisor, until finally reaching the one you need, after losing an hour and most of your sanity, shouldn't be fun.

Waiting in a Black-Friday-Walmart-worthy line to talk to the hotel to ask where your room service meal went shouldn't be fun. Rushing off to the buffet in a starving stupor and finding another Sale-Day-at-Walmart-worthy line shouldn't be fun.

With her, it is.

Wynona hooks her hand in mine. She wraps her lithe, pale arms around mine. And just like that, the waiting falls away in a hug, a giggle. She kisses me on the cheek and I could wait another day.

What do we even say to each other, talk about?

I couldn't tell you.

We joke, we tease, we talk, and we discuss.

About the line and the violently sneezing lady with the big hair trying to pass her caged growling baby tiger off as an emotional support animal. About how, even half-consciously, Wynona manages to scribble illustrations that are pure gold on the scrap of a receipt she found in her pocket. About net neutrality and what it will all come to—how the average person not knowing about it is shitty.

She makes the mundane exciting. The average anything but. And the exciting, the fun? She makes it out of this world.

I almost don't take the call when my phone rings.

"Bad news," Landon says.

"Now's not really the time," I say.

"Yes, it is," Wynona says firmly.

Her gesture to the long-ass line that's moving like an old turtle is convincing. I can't really say I don't have the time right now.

"All right," I tell Landon. "What's up?"

"Did you do something to piss off your ex?" he asks.

"She came all the way here to the hotel," I admit. "I sent her packing. Firmly, but politely enough. Why?"

Landon sighs. "I told you Marla had crazy eyes."

"Mary," I correct him. "Why is it no one could ever remember her goddamn name?"

"Because we didn't want to." A bit of typing sounds in the background—Landon's probably trying to get some emails out of his way while on the call. "She wasn't exactly model girlfriend material."

"Right, but what's up?" I say.

Even Wynona in my arms and the sexy little red Spanish dress she's wearing can't stamp out the tension that's coiled every muscle in my body. I need to know.

"It could be worse," Landon says diplomatically.

"Landon."

"Hold on, it's Kyra." More muffled now, he's probably covering the phone. "Yeah, yeah, hun. Okay, see you soon!"

"She's going to the grocery store," he explains.

"Wonderful," I say. "Now, you going to tell me?"

He makes a noncommittal grunt. "I don't want to ruin your vacation. You'll be back in a few days, anyway."

My laugh is so loudly exasperated that a bland looking girl ahead of us in line turns to shoot me an unimpressed look.

"Then why call me at all?" I demand. "But I'm not coming back in a few days."

Wynona's hand in mine, so soft and gentle, tracing circles with the pad of her thumb in my palm, doesn't calm me down. Nothing short of a full bottle of whiskey would at this point. What the fuck did Mary do?

"We decided to extend our vacation," I explain.

Another grunt. "Can you change it back?"

"No," I growl. "And I wouldn't if I could."

"All right. I should probably just tell you."

"No shit."

"Don't take that tone with me," he growls. "I was trying to look out for you."

"By calling me up to tell me that my ex is on the warpath but not telling me how?"

"Kyra thought I should tell you," he grumbles. "It wasn't my idea."

"Okay," I say.

He sighs. "It's your car."

"No," I say. "I had it parked—"

"In your building's basement parking garage, I know. There's video camera footage and everything. But we think she wore a black hoodie—original, I know—and went to town on your car with a crowbar. By the time the security guard ran out... it was too late."

"Shit." I scowl. "At least I have insurance."

"That's the thing." Landon already sounds apologetic. "Apparently, you called and converted your plan to practically nothing. Basically, the lowest you can get with it still being legal."

Shock hits me like a baseball glove around my throat.

"Emerson?" he says.

"I didn't—"

"We know," he says, sounding tired enough for the both of us. "And we tried explaining that to your insurance company, but it's no dice. They refuse to do anything, at least not until you go talk to them in person. Same with the police."

For a few seconds, the only word that can come to mind is, "Fuck..."

"I'm sorry," Landon continues.

"But what makes you think it was Mary if whoever did it wore a hoodie?" I ask.

"Whoever it was scratched out THAT'S WHAT YOU GET. You made any other enemies lately?"

My teeth grit. I have to loosen my grip on Wynona so my fingers don't dig into her. "No. Just the one. Damn it, she was right here and... I guess she got some guy to make that call to change my insurance?"

"That's what we're thinking," Landon says. "Though the police should be able to make more out of it than us. It's a real mess."

"Shit," I say.

"Yeah."

I stand there, thinking.

Wynona's blue eyes are wide with concern, but I'll explain everything to her soon enough.

Right now, I have to make a decision.

One that doesn't require much thought. I've made up my mind already.

"My car can wait an extra week," I tell Landon. "The plane tickets can't be changed anyway."

Which isn't necessarily untrue. Or true.

I just haven't checked.

"Emerson—" Landon starts.

"I've made up my mind," I say. "Thanks for letting me know. But I'm not changing my plans."

"Just think about it," he says finally, probably having caught the stubborn Storm note in my voice.

"I will," I say. "Talk later."

After I hang up, I quickly relay everything to Wynona, whose eyes widen with every new revelation.

"Jesus," she says at the end, clasping me tighter. "I'm so sorry."

"Don't be," I say. "It's my fault—and Mary's. I should've caught on to how she was earlier. Everyone else seemed to."

Wynona casts a wistful glance my way. "When we care about someone, we often see only what we want to."

I look away angrily. "But that's just it. I thought I was crazy about her all that time, but when I met you…" I exhale. "I remembered what being crazy about someone actually felt like."

"Ooh, you," she says happily.

She moves a little closer, hooking her fingers through the belt loops of my jeans as she gets a vague look in her eyes. "Sometimes, we wait so long for the person that when an almost comes around, or even less, we jump into it. We stick around as it goes from bad to worse. We make-believe our way through it until we're stuck or they leave or we do and we promise to learn from it, only the loneliness is so very scary sometimes…"

At the last part, her voice drops to a murmur, more to herself than me.

She rests her eyes on me as if remembering that I'm here. "I was really good that first year, you know. Got myself back together again. And you know what did it?"

I look at her and shake my head.

She lets go of my belt loops and smiles a smile that would be ugly on anyone else. "Rage. Revenge. I wanted to get myself so together, it'd make you so very sorry. Make you regret what you did. And it worked. I got my business together in less than six months. Got my dog and had him housebroken in a week. It was all going well until Josie thought I was well enough to be set up with a friend's brother. And then…"

She frowns and straightens. "It wasn't her fault. I should've been okay by then, ready. It had been a year since you and I had broken up. I'd gotten used to being alone, had actually come to enjoy it. All that time for my hobbies. Eating alone at restaurants like some mysterious madam. But then the dating started, and I couldn't seem to stop it. I'd get over a new guy by falling for the next. I never really liked them all that much once I got to know them, not really." She gives her head a little shake, forces a smile. "It doesn't matter now, anyway."

I take her hand. "I get it."

She quirks an unconvinced eyebrow at me. "Really."

I nod. "I used to go stir-crazy if I was alone two nights in a row. I'd call up my brothers, friends, anyone I could to go out with me. At the club, I'd end up with some girl whose name I couldn't even remember. We'd go through the motions. I'd wonder if this was all there is."

By now, we've given up on the line for the buffet. We head back to our rooms to find that room service has finally delivered.

While we sit at the table in the corner of my room and eat broiled sausages and potato wedges, Wynona bites her lip.

"What?" I say.

"I never thought it was like that for guys," she admits.

"Never thought what was?"

God, she looks pretty right now in that dress. If we weren't eating, then I'd...

"I thought hooking up was all fun for them."

I shrug. "It can be. You feel like a badass when you get her in bed, but... when it's almost every weekend or near about... it gets old."

Wynona's been chewing that sausage for way longer than necessary.

"What is it?" I ask.

"Just..." She chuckles a bit self-consciously. "It's not important."

I shrug.

She glares at me, then sighs. "I just always wondered if there was something wrong with me. Something everyone else had that I was missing." Her eyes narrow a little. "They always made it seem so fun, hooking up. Like a big ha-ha, no big deal. Like this in-joke all the cool kids knew." She looks away. "But when I tried it, it felt...

horrendous. Empty. Like two bodies I had no acquaintance with rubbing together. Like animals. Like two sex dolls at a shop, two robots, two…"

Her shoulders are bunched up, and I cover them with my palms. "Hey… it's okay. I'm here now." I pat her head against my chest. "It's okay."

Her face is grimaced. "It's not, though. You want to know what kind of original I am, Emerson? I was so sure I just needed to be different, just needed to be more like them. I just needed to care less and have fun more and let loose. You remember, our parents were really strict, mine and Josie's, an old-fashioned pair. I thought they didn't have a clue. So, I tried it, piss-drunk, and it was the worst night of my life."

I stroke her head. "Hey… It's okay."

She digs her forehead into my chest. "But it's not, Emerson, don't you get it? I was lying there, with my mind screaming at me, Please stop, please don't do this, please, please, will you just stop, I'll do anything if you'll just stop. And I didn't. Because I wanted it to stop hurting so much. I wanted to stop caring so much. I wanted to believe them, to get it. And even after, when I went through the charade with boyfriends like so many cards in a deck, talking more but saying less. Both of us aware, in some foggy back-part of our mind, that we were placeholders, patches for broken hearts that couldn't work right."

"Wyn…" I say, more than helpless, useless.

Her eyes fill with tears as she looks at me. "So, if you're wondering who I am, Emerson Storm, it's that. Someone lonely and pathetic who makes bad decisions."

"Why?" is all I can think to say. "Why are you telling me all this?"

"Because I've never told anyone, and because if I didn't, it would wait, and I would be scared of ruining things."

"Why would it ruin anything?"

"Why wouldn't it?"

I take both of her hands and clasp them, clasp them hard. "You don't get it."

She looks away. I turn her head back to face me.

"Wyn. I like you—not what you've done or who you've been. I like you now. Here. That's not going to change, whatever happened."

Her eyes look like they want to believe. "Even if I can't trust you, can't trust myself?"

I shrug. "Maybe you shouldn't for now. If you've let yourself down, since I've let you down, it only makes sense that you wouldn't trust yourself or trust me. You'll have to earn your trust back. I will too. We will. Together."

I put an arm around her and look at her. "Will you do that with me?"

Her breathing is soft and quiet. Her back is still tensed.

But then she breathes, "Yes..." into my shoulder and pulls up to peer into my eyes, and I know.

Everything is going to be all right.

CHAPTER 17

Wynona

I go to bed feeling warm and safe next to Emerson and wake up feeling ice-cold and sick on the opposite side of the bed.

Sweat slicks my face. There are no sheets on me. My stomach is contracting, long fingernails of pain scraping me from the inside.

I totter to the bathroom just in time.

Not again...

Oh, yes, again.

As I empty my stomach and stay there, on my knees, on the cool tile floor, my mind does some vain flutterings. Trying to figure it out all.

Could it be food poisoning?

Possibly, only I've had a stomach notoriously impervious to it all my life. Even in Cancun, when every member of my family and even a few of the staff got it and were fighting over the few bathrooms, I was fine.

Unless...

I check my phone hurriedly for the app that reminds me.

No. Fucking. Way.

But there it is, on a phone screen that doesn't care what I want. Three days. My period was supposed to start three days ago.

Josie's isn't so regular. Sierra's wasn't until she got her IUD a few years back. But mine? Same start day. Every time.

I've never missed a period until now.

Which means...

I throw on a bathrobe and scuttle out of the room, back to my own room.

I can explain to Emerson later. "Just felt sick, ugh". If it is only that.

"Please, God, let it be that," I mutter, half under my breath.

Reaching my room, I swipe myself in, then collapse onto the bed. The world is spinning. My stomach is acting like I never threw up and it needs to up the ante to clue me in.

I do the only thing I can do.

"This had better be good," Josie grumbles when she answers the door. "I was having this really good dream… living in this castle with so many plants, prayer plants and monsteras, birds of paradise and pileas—"

"I think I might be pregnant," I blurt out.

"Oh," she says, gaping at me. "Okay. That's fair."

"That's fair?" I sputter. "Josie, did you hear me?"

"I don't know what to say," she admits with a grimace. "Why do you think that?"

"My period, I'm never late," I moan. "And I can't stop throwing up."

"Jesus," Josie says. "Did you take a pregnancy test?"

"Not yet," I say.

"Well, you'd better."

"No shit, Sherlock."

"Whoa, I'm just trying to help here."

I sigh. "I know, Jos. I'm sorry. I'm just freaking out here."

"I don't blame you. Have you told Emerson?"

"Are you kidding? Things have actually been going super well. This is the last thing either of us needs."

"Need or not," Josie says, "you have to find out. ASAP. And then…"

"Do not say 'and then'," I groan. "I'm in no state to even begin to think about that."

"Sorry," Josie says.

"It's okay," I say.

Silence, while my thoughts ram against the sides of my head. How can this be happening? What am I going to do?

"So," Josie says. "Do you want to talk? I can be here for you if you need."

Oh, right.

It's a measure of how freaking out I am that I didn't realize it's the middle of the night, and my poor sister wants some sleep.

"I'm good," I say. "I'll go see if the hotel's pharmacy is open. Take that pregnancy test."

"Feel free to have me come along, or let me know when you get the results," Josie says with a sigh. "I probably won't be having that plant castle dream again anyway."

I snort. "Fingers crossed for you."

"Nah," Josie says. "Fingers crossed for you. Good luck—and good night!"

The next few minutes are painful. My head is pierced with the beginnings of a headache, my stomach is rumbling with WWIII, and every one of my muscles feels like it's groaning as I pull on some decent clothes to get to the pharmacy.

I may be distraught and possibly pregnant, but I'm not going to wander in there dressed like a complete invalid.

The pharmacy is, thank God, open. The frizzy-haired woman there looks at me as if I did stroll in wearing the hotel's soft white bathrobe. Then again, she probably doesn't get many customers at two AM or whatever time it is.

It takes me way longer than necessary to find the thing. Mainly because I'm stubborn and embarrassed and the assortment of items appears to be completely random. There's one brand of charcoal toothpaste right beside banana-flavored condoms, while a kids' toothpaste on the opposite side of the room is next to a 'Get Well Soon' card with a fat, sympathetic-looking duck on it. When I finally find the way-too-cheery pink pregnancy kit box, wedged between Aero bars and granny panty underwear, I grab it and head for the cash register.

The frizzy woman's sneer doesn't change at the sight of my purchase, which makes me think that maybe that's just her face.

I stash the thing in my purse and hurry back to my room furtively, like it's eight grams of cocaine instead of a simple pregnancy test.

Inside my room, I look my door. I check my phone. I peer through the balcony's sliding glass door at the impartial night outside.

But finally, I can't avoid it any longer. I take out the tester with shaking hands.

Please, God, or Jesus or Buddha, or whoever the hell, please.

I swallow and stride to the bathroom.

Inside, I sit on the cool toilet seat and force myself to exhale. And then I pee and stick the test in.

Afterward, I put it in the sink and wait.

Way more than a minute passes. I try to come up with something—anything—to avoid looking at it. But I need to know.

I grab it, look at it, and let it drop to the floor.

No.

Oh, hell no.

Wobbly legs take me to the bed and keep me there.

My gaze follows along the designs on the ceiling while my mind runs wild.

So, this is what it's like when your whole world changes. When your life as you know it is over.

I should tell Josie. I should go to her and tell her and have her calming voice figure out what to do.

But I can't. Won't.

Telling Josie will make it more real. Saying the words out loud...

I can't. Not yet.

Jesus, how did this even happen?

I take the pill religiously. Josie is the one who's always forgetting and giggling about it—"Whoopsie!"—on vacations and crazy nights out.

But me? I always take it.

I. Never. Miss. A. Pill.

Not that it matters now.

I can't keep it. I can't get rid of it either.

I turn on my side, closing my eyes, willing sleep to come.

Some days, some situations, the only thing that can make it better is the ultimate form of escape—sleep.

**

In my dream, I'm a giraffe. I have the longest neck imaginable, so gloriously long that it stretches all the way into the puffy clouds. I smile at the banana moon and the pumpkin-sized planets, my friends. The stars feel like sprinklers when I pass my head through them. They smell like bubble gum.

Only, someone's got a chisel and is hammering away at the moon!

Knock, knock, knock... knock, knock, knock...

My eyes open.

"Wynona?" Emerson says from outside the door.

I stagger over to it.

My hand meets the cool of the handle when I remember.

"Hey," I say.

"What's up? Can I come in?"

Yes, my heart says.

No, my head says.

"No, I... I'm not feeling well," I say. "Sorry I just left like that. I threw up."

"Damn. Need to see a doctor?"

"No... I–I'm just going to go to bed," I tell him. "I'll call you later."

A pause, then, "You sure that you don't want me with you?"

"No, I'm... not that bad. Just need to sleep it off, I think. Bye."

And then I go back to my bed before my strength fails me.

Because I want to see him. I want to touch him, hold him, smell him. I want those strong arms to wrap around me with the certainty that everything's going to be okay.

But I can't. Not now.

I can't hold it together now.

So, I go back to bed and let the tears come and hope that sleep does, too.

I wake up sometime later to more knocking. I ignore it and go back to sleep again.

The next time I wake up, it's my phone. I try turning it off but end up inadvertently answering it.

"Go away, Emerson," I mumble.

"Oh, so you're avoiding him?" Josie says. "Shit, Wyn. Are you? And me? I've tried stopping by your room a couple of times."

I exhale the word: "Yep."

"Oh, Jesus."

"I know," I say.

"What are you going to do?"

"No idea."

Background noises. Josie's probably doing one of those brisk walks she always liked doing back home.

Back home… where I should be. Who knows, maybe if I hadn't stayed on, stayed longer here, if I'd just gone home how I should've, then none of this would've happened.

If I'd just made that goddamn plane…

"Have you told him?" she asks quietly.

"No."

"When are you going to?"

"I don't know, Jos. Okay? This is a lot to process. I haven't even decided what I'm going to do yet."

Josie's silent, and still, I find myself annoyed.

With her, with my own bitchy tone.

"Just say it," I snap.

"Well, you should tell him," she argues. "You don't know. Maybe this wouldn't mess things up how you think."

There she is again. Josie Pollyanna Collins, eternal optimist. I could almost laugh—if I wasn't sure that it would end in tears, that is.

"Get real," I find myself snapping. "Emerson and I aren't some tried-and-true couple thinking of settling down. We're two exes who are still figuring out what the hell is going on. We've been together less than two weeks. Of course it will mess things up."

Josie doesn't say anything.

"I should go," I say.

"Wait," she says. "I want to be there for you. If you need me. Want me to head to your room now?"

"No," I say, suddenly very, very tired. "I just need to be alone right now and figure this one out on my own."

She doesn't ask the question hanging over us like a giant boulder ready to fall. How?

"Bye, Josie," I say. "Thanks for checking in."

"Wyn," she says, "let's talk about this. Why don't I head to your room and we can—"

"I can't," I say simply. "Not yet. Bye."

And then I hang up, lie back down, and hope for more sleep.

At least some wishes come true...

By the time I finally wake up, it's night out, nine PM.

My phone has a message from Emerson—How are you?—that I don't answer.

I feel like I could still sleep some more, but right now, between weariness and hunger, my growling stomach wins out.

I head to the buffet amid blah-faced hotel guests whose moods finally seem to match mine. I pick over whatever's still left in the metal pans, some mashed-up hash browns, a dubiously-crisped piece of bacon.

On my way back, I can't help it. I stop by Josie's room, but she's not in. Then, I stop by his room.

He opens the door. When he sees me, his face can't decide whether to be happy or guarded. He knows something is up. "Hey."

"Hey," I say.

"You feeling better?"

"Mostly. Sorry I was so grumpy before."

He shrugs. "No worries. You should see Nolan when he has a cold." He shudders.

I chuckle. "That bad?"

Emerson's grinning and grimacing at the same time. "Worse. He'll cocoon himself in so many blankets that he looks like a sumo wrestler, then moan and whine for chicken noodle soup and whiskey every five minutes."

"Whiskey?" I ask.

Emerson, still chuckling, just shrugs. "Jax, his best friend, is part Irish and swears by it for knocking out any sickness. Though I think it just plain knocks you out."

I chuckle. "Sounds about right."

Emerson's gaze dips to my plate and its pathetic contents. "The selection at the buffet's that bad?"

"Worse," I say. "I'm pretty sure I saw two kids fighting over a slice of rotten cantaloupe."

"Damn," he says, scowling and taking my plate. "You shouldn't be eating this. Especially if you've been feeling sick. Let me take you out."

"I don't know…"

"Why not?" he asks.

"I…" I trail off.

Why not? Because I'm worried I'll get too close to you again and blurt out everything before I'm ready.

"All right," I say instead. "But I'm changing first. Give me ten minutes."

Back in my room, luckily, the sickness is mostly gone. Maybe because it's been replaced by a different, deeper sort of sickness.

That of a ticking clock that will eventually have to stop. A secret with a time limit.

Minutes after I'm ready and dressed in a knee-length dress that is neither fancy nor casual, I stare at my reflection.

Well, you should tell him. Maybe this wouldn't mess things up how you think.

Who knows? Josie could be right.

Thing is, it would change things. It couldn't not.

And I don't want them to be changed, not yet.

Right now, things are still a bit scary and a lot new. But low pressure. We aren't around friends or family. In a way, we aren't even in the real world.

We're in this tropical bubble where the temperature is as warm and easy as we are.

Breaking the news to Emerson… would be like jumping out of paradise. And that's something I'm not willing to do.

Not yet, at least.

I meet Emerson at the lobby steps, as agreed. We take one look at each other, then another outside.

I've been so involved with my thoughts and the shit-I'm-pregnant thing that I hadn't even noticed.

It's pouring out.

Rain.

Big, cold gobs of it that I know from experience hit you like a kamikaze bee. Mini-rivers of it rush down the sides of the roads.

Thunder crackles further off.

"Your choice," Emerson says, gesturing into the deluge. "The place is close enough to walk. I'd rather taxi, but up to you."

"Is that a joke?" I say, holding out a bare arm hesitantly as the droplets splatter down. "Taxi, of course."

"Atta girl," Emerson says.

He manages to wrap his arms around me and wave down a taxi that's been idling around the hotel's entry roundabout at the same time.

As we step inside, I take another glance at the storm and shudder.

"What if I had said walk?" I ask Emerson once we're inside the scratchy-seat taxi.

He squeezes my hand, making a face. "Guess I would've grinned and borne it. And run like hell."

"I'm not very fast," I say with a chuckle.

He steals a kiss. "Then I would've picked you up."

With our faces so close like this, I can see all the details you normally wouldn't. The stray freckle near the corner of his right eye. The lightest of smile marks on his jawline. A small sandy patch of quarter-inch-long hairs just under his chin that he must've missed when shaving.

He smells like a cologne that makes me want to bury my face into his chest and not come out.

We're so close like this, so near, that it makes me a bit self-conscious.

Like he's sure to notice the ugly scar on my chin from when Josie and I were having a flipping contest on the trampoline and I bashed my face on the side. Or how I messed up the line of my cat eye in the middle of my left eye. Or how I'm already getting a slight wrinkle between my eyebrows from the frustrated face I apparently always make.

Or even that I'm keeping something from him.

I look away just as we pull up to the restaurant.

I have to laugh. "Wow, it really was close."

"You bet," Emerson says, getting out first and hurriedly taking something out of his pocket as he comes around to the door on my side.

Seconds later, he's unfurling an umbrella and gesturing for me to come under it.

"You're all prepared, aren't you?" I ask.

He just smiles.

We hurry to the door, Emerson careful to keep the umbrella covering me completely. He holds the door while I head inside.

One look around, and I already like this place. It's covered—as in, floor to ceiling, wall to window covered—with masks. Dark wood masks, ebony masks, masks painted bright garish colors, masks with big gaping holes for eyes, masks with crooked jack-o'-lantern mouths. It even smells of wood, rich and musty. The one thing that's keeping this ode to masks from being a bit creepy is the presence of exotic plants. Pothos and philodendron thread among the masks, lush and expansive, so easily that part of me has to wonder if the masks are some sort of fertilizer. I'm probably being ridiculous.

"I hope there are no curses on any of these," I lean in to whisper to Emerson with a chuckle.

He wraps an arm around me. "Don't worry, I'll protect you."

Our waiter is already arriving, a lean man who could be anywhere from twenty to forty. He takes us to a table by the window.

One look outside, at the deluge still going on, makes me breathe a sigh of relief. My gaze wanders and stops on a funny mask just beside me—it has cartoonish, bulging painted eyes paired with a droll little mouth that doesn't seem to match.

"Wine would be nice to start out with, don't you think?" Emerson asks, a wooden slab of a menu already in hand.

"No," I blurt out.

When he looks up, surprised, I quickly improvise. "I think, with how sick I was… it's better to hold off for a bit."

How about nine months, to be exact?

Kill. Me. Now.

Emerson's glance flickers back to the menu. "Makes sense. I won't make you suffer seeing me enjoy myself, then. We should try some of their homemade mango juice."

"Sounds good to me," I say.

As the night goes on, I find myself relaxing bit by bit. After all, there's no huge rush to tell Emerson.

I can let us enjoy ourselves for the next week, then go home, see what happens, and get some perspective on this all. Even without getting pregnant, this has all been such a crazy whirlwind.

It wouldn't hurt to take a breather.

It's so easy to be with Emerson, most of all tonight.

If he notices the admiring gazes some of the swankily half-dressed gorgeous women here shoot him, he gives no sign. As for me, when I chat with a man at the bar on my way to the bathroom, before I know it, Emerson's there, introducing himself. "Emerson. Wynona's boyfriend."

Back at our table, I almost grin. "What was that all about?"

Emerson shrugs.

"Okay..." I say.

His look cuts to me. "I'm not one to not let you go out with your girlfriends dancing or anything overprotective like that, but if a man tries to chat you up when I'm in the room, I'm going to make sure that he knows where we stand. That okay?"

"Yeah," I say. "Cool if I do it too?"

He smirks, taking my hand. "Knock yourself out. Before, it was my brothers steering me away from sketchy women, but feel free to take that up if you want. My brothers don't have time anymore, with kids and all."

"Kids," I say, a tremor going through me at the word. I should leave it at that, let it be, but I can't. Something nameless is impelling me on. "It seems so crazy that people our age have them. I feel like I only recently got the hang of looking after myself... let alone a child."

Emerson nods. "It's a huge responsibility. I don't know how they do it—balance the work, a relationship with their partner, and the kid. Not sure I could."

"Could," I ask lightly, "Or would?"

Emerson shrugs. "Either? I wouldn't say never, but I'm definitely not where I'd want to be for a kid to come into the picture."

A twitch goes through me.

And there it is, Wynona, what you knew he'd say, what you practically goaded him into saying, what he most definitely did say.

"Wyn?" he asks, taking my hand.

"Sorry, just lost in thought," I say, flashing a smile.

"I asked, what about you?"

"Same here," I sing-song. "Last thing I need right now is a child."

The last thing I need, and the first thing I have... the last thing I need, and the last thing I want, and exactly what I have... a kid... a kid... a goddamn kid.

"Wynona?" Emerson's holding both of my hands now, peering into my face with concern. "You okay? You look kind of peaked."

I rise. "I'm fine. I'll just go splash some cold water on my face."

I almost say that I've been getting hot flashes, but that's stupid and ridiculous because it's not like I'm menopausal. Just freaking the fuck out.

In the bathroom, the soap smells like grapefruit if you pared down the sweetest parts of five different ones. The mirror is ringed by, you guessed it, more masks, with increasingly mocking expressions. But the only face I have eyes for is the one in the mirror.

"You can do this," I tell her. "Let's do this."

So, I go out and do it.

I eat the rest of my meal—some weird-named fish with weirder-named spices on it with some fiddleheads and homemade bread. I chat with Emerson some more as if nothing in the world is wrong, no, nothing. And then we go back to the hotel, and I pretend to be tired, and we sleep, but not in each other's arms because I pretend to be asleep when really, I'm afraid.

Afraid of what I'm carrying. Afraid of what it'll mean, what it'll force us to do. Afraid of getting too close to this man, who hurt me before, and being forced to tell him what will force him to hurt me again.

When he thinks I'm asleep, I can feel Emerson run his hand down my body softly. Into my neck, he whispers, "Tomorrow. You're going to love it. You'll see."

CHAPTER 18

Emerson

Before she wakes up, I check my bank account online.

The numbers don't lie. It doesn't look good.

Staying at this hotel longer was already a splurge, and these past few nights, the boat... it's hit my account hard.

Hard enough that if I keep this up, I'll have to dip into my savings.

Shit.

"What you looking at?" Wynona says sleepily from the bed.

"Damn it, caught in the act," I joke, going over to snuggle in next to her.

"Emerson?" she says after a minute or so of cuddling.

Yep. Not going to get out of it that easily.

"My bank account," I admit. "Not a big deal."

"Then why do you look all tense?" she asks, snuggling into my arms and gazing up at my face.

"I'll just have to pick up a few more concerts to play at when I get back," I say. "It'll be fine."

She bites her lip, looking down. "And you're sure that you shouldn't have taken..."

"That again?" I growl, sitting up straight and letting her go. "I thought we were past that."

Her glare is fierce. "I just don't want you to be hard up and make some decision you'll regret later."

"Hey." I take her hand in mine. It's funny, I keep forgetting how small it is. "I chose you. I'm not going to regret that."

She just keeps looking down, nods a little. I tip her chin up so she's facing me. "Understand?"

Suddenly, she grins, stealing a kiss. "Understood."

We have a nice, still-sleepy quickie in bed.

"What were you saying last night?" she asks afterward as we get dressed.

I frown humorously at her. "When you were supposed to be asleep, you mean?"

That grin of hers... two parts naughty, one part repentant. "Okay, got me."

"I'll tell you over breakfast," I say, taking her hand.

I end up telling her on the way back. "I rented us an island for tonight."

She drops my hand, glaring even more fiercely at me. "Emerson!"

"Sorry?"

Her glare doesn't budge. "One minute you're admitting that money is an issue, and the next you're splurging on something like that?"

I take her hand firmly. "I paid for it before I checked my accounts this morning. And there's no refund. So, you can refuse to come, but it'll just be wasting money that's already been paid."

She glares at me for a bit longer before finally sighing. "All right. If you say so."

"I'm a grown man, Wynona," I growl. "It's time you started treating me like it."

Mouth open, face apparently about to deliver another scolding, she pauses, then nods. "You're right. I just... worry about you."

"Leave that to me," I say more gently. "Okay?"

"Okay," she agrees. "When do we set out for this island?"

"As soon as you can get packed up," I tell her.

Half an hour later, we're meeting at the back entrance of the hotel, the one that leads to the beach.

"I'm actually pretty excited," Wynona confesses as we head to my boat. "I've never stayed on a private island before."

"Me too," I tell her.

This time, on the boat, I don't spend time enjoying the view. I consult the map provided by the Airbnb island owners and set sail. One brief conversation with Wynona later, and we're there.

Wynona steps onto the sandy beach with a growing smile. "We're here."

"That we are," I agree, taking her bag and hitching it onto my shoulder before she can protest.

Although she does frown at me. "I'm not an invalid, you know."

I let my gaze linger on her how it wanted to for the whole boat ride. "No, you're in damn good shape."

She gives me a playful whack. "Perv."

I just shrug. "Just noticing the obvious."

"We should work out together sometime," Wynona says.

"I'd like that," I say. "I'm pretty sure Greyson mentioned that our hotel has a great gym, though I haven't checked it out myself. And back home, too."

"Yeah, back home," she says, trying to smile, a vague look coming into her eyes.

Probably just nerves.

It seems like the past few days, whenever I've mentioned 'back home', something has been off about Wynona.

Fuck if I know, though.

"So, what happens now?" she asks once we've unloaded our stuff into the pretty cabin further inland.

I unzip a bag and take out the snorkel gear. "Snorkeling?"

Wynona's eyes light up as she throws her arms around me. "You think of everything!"

I wrap my arms around her, not mentioning how she told me that she'd never been a few days ago.

The next hour consists of getting on the gear, making out a little after Wynona changes into her hot little teal bikini—how the hell am I supposed to help it when she looks that good?—then dipping our heads under the just-right water and checking out the underwater world down there.

"I can't believe there's so much down there!" Wynona exclaims after our first head dip.

She's right, too. Coral and fish of every color, shape, and size seem to be there. The crystalline water is easy to see through, too.

Late that night, after we've explored the sand-and palm tree-covered island from one shore to the other, Wynona cooks the pork chops I brought as a thank you. Then, we eat and sit in the swing that overlooks a tiny cliff overlooking the water on the opposite side of the island.

"This place is amazing," Wynona says, snuggling her head into mine, her whole body a study in contentment. For just a glimpse of her like this, I'd do it all again. "Thank you."

"No, thank you," I reply. "For the pork. Wouldn't have tasted that good if I'd made it."

Wynona pats me with a lazy smile. "Well, you can't be good at everything."

I kiss the top of her head. "Oh, yeah?"

She turns into my lips with a "Yeah."

Our kiss is nice. Slow.

Those pillows of her lips. How her whole body is leaning into me. Goddamn.

The kiss develops. Soon, our hands are all over each other, stroking, unbuttoning, undoing.

She's wearing that teal cartoon cherry bikini I can't get enough of. I thumb her breasts over the swimsuit cups, enjoying the hard nubs of her nipples before I dip my thumbs underneath. Then my hands.

Fucking hell, her breasts are perfect. So soft. Smooth. Full. Pert.

One hand enjoys one while my other hand enjoys the other.

Our lips meet again. Her hands are running along my shoulders, my back, my front, then... there.

"Someone's excited," she murmurs, pulling away with a smirk.

I take the back of her head and press her face back to mine. Then I press my own hand in between her legs. She's wet, and the last time we swam was hours ago.

She kisses me hard and rough and rubs her hands painstakingly along my cock.

"That's it," I growl after a few minutes.

I yank off my briefs, and then her bikini, and then pull her to me.

Our kiss picks up where it left off, deepens. Our bodies ease together.

Fuck. I'm so close.

So fucking close.

My cock noses at her entrance, around it.

We both groan.

Another stab and I'm in partway.

So warm... tight... and warm... fucking hell.

A pussy better than all others.

Our kiss twists, pulls away, and then everything is in my next thrust. Dipping into her deeper...

...and deeper.

...and deeper.

And all at once, as we quiver together, it's not enough. Not nearly e-fucking-nough.

Our pelvises are pounding together—"More, Emerson."—needing more upon more. Faster. Harder. Better.

Until she's crying out, trembling so beautifully in my arms, her glossy dark-haired head thrown back, throat bared as she comes.

Afterward, I hold her trembling form, my fingertips idling over her breasts, her ass.

Her half-lidded eyes are a deeper blue than I've ever seen them. She looks at me. "You."

I press a kiss into her soft forehead. "You."

Her lips part, then smirk, as if from some secret thought.

"What?" I say.

She presses her ass into me. "Fuck me again."

Just like that, I'm instantly hard. I kiss her harder, all the way to the sandy ground. We're grabbing and stroking and kissing and pressing against each other all at once, furiously.

I'm back inside her, deep inside her. Jackhammering her furiously. Her pussy is clasping for my cock as fast and as hard as I'm pounding her.

In and out. In and deeper and out.

Until she's coming, and I'm coming, losing it inside that beautiful, sweet pussy of hers.

Fuck yeah…

Afterward, we lie on the grass and look up at the stars.

It's quiet out, save the soft beat of the waves. Like even the world is sleeping too.

The breeze is cool on my skin, Wynona a warm blanket.

"Want to know what I think?" Wynona says suddenly.

CHAPTER 19

Wynona

"What?" Emerson asks.

My mouth opens and the words won't come out. There's something you should know.

So, instead, I say the only ones I can bear to say. "I think it's time to go to sleep."

Emerson gives my butt a little squeeze. "Oh, yeah?"

No.

No, I don't want to. I want to lie here with you and tell you that I'm pregnant with our child.

I want to tell you everything.

But I don't.

Instead, I kiss him like there's nothing the matter and rise, taking his hand.

That night, I don't sleep much. The bed is comfortable. I've never been safer than when I'm in Emerson's arms.

And yet, what I haven't told him is as good as a shot of caffeine at keeping me awake.

How long can I keep it to myself?

I thought waiting longer would make me feel more ready. But if anything, the closer we get, the less ready I feel.

I practice it out in my head. Hey, there's something I need to tell you. I'm pre—okay, there's something I've been meaning to tell you. I'm—

But every time, even my mind stumbles over the words.

The words that could change everything.

Finally, I'm tired of my own melodramatics and fall asleep out of sheer frustration.

The next morning, I wake up to a delicious smell.

"Rise and shine," Emerson says, coming onto the bed beside me with a platter loaded with two food-heaped plates. "Or I'll eat all this myself."

"Jerk," I mumble sleepily.

Emerson slips a piece of bacon between my lips. "Still a jerk?"

I take an experimental bite—holy yumminess—then sigh. "Okay, maybe not."

Emerson snorts as I wrestle myself upright. "Maybe?"

He hands me a plate, and I take another bite. "Okay, definitely not. Though you should know by now that I'm not a morning person."

Emerson smirks. "Oh, good. I was taking all those death threats personally."

We crack up as we dig in.

"You want a good mood in the morning, you should try Josie," I continue as we eat. "The girl actually sings and does house chores first thing."

Emerson slings me a sidelong glance as he finishes up his toast. "And you two are related."

"Only twins," I say with an offhand shrug.

We chuckle.

"I used to wish I had one," Emerson admits, staring off. "Nolan and Landon, they seemed so good together. Just a pair. Yeah, they fought and sometimes pulled these awful pranks on each other, but at the end of the day, they were best friends. The best. Greyson was already independent, even back then. Nolan and Landon had each other, and I had my music." He shrugs. "Not a bad setup, I guess."

"See, when I was a kid, I hated having a twin," I admit with a lopsided smile. "Not Josie—trying to hate her is like trying to hate chocolate, basically impossible. It was the twin thing itself that drove me nuts—us always being compared to each other, always being measured up against each other. She always got to be the happy twin, the fun twin, the well-adjusted twin, and I was... whatever was left."

Emerson gently takes my hand. "What was?"

I shrug, then gesture to myself with a wry laugh. "Whatever this is."

"Good," he says simply.

I stare at him.

For saying something so simple, so perfect, that I never would've thought or expected it myself.

Not a compelling argument, not a list of reasons. Just a statement of truth that one glance at him reveals he meant.

We eat the rest of the meal in silence. Although it's a silence all its own.

Not a silence brimming with the unsaid, loud with inferences. Not even a silence wondering what to say next and when.

Just the comfortable silence you see in movies or read about in books and think doesn't exist until it does for you. And then, you understand it and that there's no explaining it.

Might as well try to explain hope to a parrot, freedom to a blade of grass.

We get our stuff packed up and head to Emerson's boat. The view of the water and the shore as we get on the boat is the kind they use on desktop and phone wallpapers, the water an impossible blue, the sky a similar shade. The suggestion of a shore on the horizon, which I know is closer than it looks.

For most of the boat ride, I almost don't think of it. I almost lose myself in the easy chatting with Emerson, the rhythmic vibrations of the boat, the sweep of sea air in my nostrils. Almost.

But… maybe it's the sight of the growing shoreline. It comes back.

What I haven't told him. What I need to.

But I don't tell him when we get off the boat and head back to our rooms with plans for later. I don't tell him after I've unpacked, showered, and gotten dressed. I don't tell him when we meet up again and go for a swim in the pool with the blue and purple artistic mosaics of mermaids and angel fish, even though we're basically alone.

I don't tell him.

Not yet.

That night, it's a calmer night than others, just us in Emerson's room, at my request. I do love my activities, but in order to enjoy them fully, I need space between them too.

And lately, I've had enough excitement to last me several months.

"This is nice," I say, relaxing my head in Emerson's lap.

"Yeah," he says, his hands idling in my hair.

He's got a look on his tanned, sculpted face that I could read a lot into if I'm not careful.

The thing is, I'm tired to death of being careful. Careful to say the right thing. Be the right person. Figure out what 'right' actually even is.

"Hang on," Emerson says, gently disengaging himself and heading to his keyboard bag.

"Seriously?" I say, half-joking.

He just grins as he gets back on the bed. He takes out the keyboard, sets it on his lap, and with one last sidelong glance my way, he starts to play.

The words come with the song, even without his singing them.

Past, present, future, you are

Whenever I'm far

… away

It's all coming back to me, like a fingertip tapping my brain in just the right place. Every day, as I ate, worked, and went through the motions of living, I waited for the minutes to click away to when I would really start to live.

Half an hour before, I'd put on makeup, choose something other than the sweats I'd been wearing all day. If I'd forgotten to wash my hair for a while, I'd put it up.

At ten PM on the dot, his call would come and ignite my beating heart. How good he looked, tousled sandy hair, shy happy smile, even with his webcam's crappy resolution. He was so close and present—even separated by a camera—that I could almost smell him, that deep musk I loved so well.

His voice was mostly untransformed by the internet connection, a deep warm baritone that made me smile even from such a mundane greeting as "Hey."

That same warm voice and I would talk about everything, but most of all, the seemingly never-ending series of concerts he was doing, part of the world tour he was on. The different countries, England and the cheese rolling competition he stumbled on in Gloucestershire. Romania and the colorful Merry Cemetery he wandered with fellow musicians in Săpânța. Japan and how a friend of his almost bought a car out of a vending machine.

We'd touch upon what was going on in my life too, of course, although I'd be careful to coat the truth—the friends I was seeing less and less of, the courses I was failing, the job to which I was calling in sick so much that they'd given me a warning—in vague platitudes he didn't see through.

We'd talk about the trips and dates and things we'd do when he got back. We'd talk about the movies we'd seen, the books we'd read and wanted to. We talked philosophy and science and spirituality and meaning.

We'd have so much to talk about, night after night after night, that we'd sometimes talk well into the next day, early morning start for our jobs be damned.

The first time he was late to our ten o'clock talk, I wrote it off as a fluke. Then came the second. Then the time he didn't call at all.

The apologies after always turned into fights.

Then, after it finally ended and we had broken up, when the hulking maw of nothingness was all that remained of what we had been, I'd reread our phone texts, our Skype chats, tried to see our future in the past. Tried to see signs that it would all fall apart. That I was a fool for ever thinking differently.

...It's time to say

I gotta get back to you

I gotta get back to you...

"Stop," I blurt out suddenly.

Emerson's hand falls still.

"Sorry," he says. "It just..."

I turn away from those guilty eyes wanting to make right what can't be.

"Happened, I know," I find myself saying. "Just like this. Us."

Just like what I still haven't told him.

"Wynona," he says, reaching for me.

I don't let him, even though I long for his hand, his touch, like a magnet to steel.

"There's something I have to tell you," I say in a voice that sounds way surer than I'm feeling.

I don't look at him. I can't.

I can't see the disappointment in his face at what I'm about to say. I can't bear it.

Emerson waits, patient.

He can afford to be.

He doesn't have the slightest idea how what I'm about to say will blow everything up, will change everything, throw the blurry into focus, force a swerving car into a specific lane.

My fists ball so much that my knuckles crack. My breath thrashes. My shoulders slump.

This is the last thing I want to do. This is what I must do.

The words come out like a curse, like a what-the-hell flip-off at fate. "I'm pregnant."

Emerson exhales sharply. "What?"

"I was getting sick, was late for my period." My voice is dull with the mercilessness of fact. "I took a test. It was positive."

I wait.

Long enough for Emerson to control whatever's happening on his face.

But when I finally have enough courage to face him, he's rising, heading for the balcony.

I watch him leave while the thoughts, circling me like vultures, finally descend.

What did you expect?

That he'd be happy? Anything other than horrified?

That he'd wrap his arms around you and lie that it was going to be okay?

I sink back on the bed and stare at the ceiling. It's a different style here, less flow and suggestion, more line and state.

How long am I going to lie here and pretend that Emerson's leaving, getting away, wasn't an answer in itself?

How long am I going to delude myself?

I sit up, rise. My eyes are blinking, my cheeks wet.

I head for the door.

"Wynona?" he says.

I pause.

"Just... can you look at me?" he asks softly.

I look at him.

Behind the tears, it takes a minute for me to make out just what's on his face. Sheer puzzlement.

"What?" I ask.

"I…" He shakes his head, scowling, annoyed. "I don't know why, but for some reason, I don't feel like this is the worst thing. I almost feel like it's… okay."

"Really?"

He nods, still with that puzzled expression that I could kiss. "Really."

He takes me in his arms and kisses me first. "One thing, though. Can you give me some time to think about this? A few days or nights should be enough. I just have to get my head around it."

"Of course." I find myself laughing. Out of all the reactions I expected and feared, this didn't factor into it. "Hell yes, of course!"

Looking at me, he starts to laugh, big booming ones that light up his whole face. "Okay."

I laugh too, I can't help it. The laughs are coming out riding on a wave of wild relief. "Okay."

And then we kiss some more, all the way back to bed.

And this time, when Emerson plays a Beatles song on his keyboard, we both sing along. "Blackbird singing in the dead of night…"

CHAPTER 20

Emerson

What. The. Fuck.

From the balcony, I stare out into night sky, smiling like a fool.

As if it had an answer for me, anything other than a nice view of the beach and further-on forest, along with a star-studded sky.

If you had asked me about babies a few hours ago, I would've chuckled and said, "Maybe someday."

But someday is… now?

Jesus, Wynona and I have barely started getting to know each other again.

My hands close on the railing.

There's the practical aspect of the whole thing, too. I'm well-off enough, but a baby needs more than that.

It needs time. Responsibility. Huge amounts of both.

And a house. Wouldn't it be needing that sooner rather than later?

And what about Wynona and me? Sure, things have been going great here on the island… but what about back home?

I give my head a swift shake.

Too many questions and not enough answers.

All I need to know now is what to tell Wynona. I stand on the balcony, looking out, until I do.

I go back to bed, and when we wake up, smiling and kissing sleepily, I have an idea. "Have you checked out the little town nearby yet? Maybe before the wedding?"

Wynona smiles as she shakes her head. "Not yet."

"You game?" I ask.

An hour later, we're walking down the town's tidy cobblestone streets. Every other block smells of cinnamon and sweet candy, while each one-story, white-doored building is a different pastel color. Storefronts brim with artisanal crafts, clothing, and the odd smiling shopkeeper.

It's almost like being in an art gallery, with all the vibrant paintings of seascapes and fish and unique sculptures of wide-hipped women with fish heads or shark fins.

"This was a good idea," Wynona says as we sit on a pink and blue polka-dot bench, sharing a chocolate-mint ice cream cone.

I take a bite, grinning. "Agreed. Ice cream is never a bad idea."

Licking a stray smear of it from her fuchsia-lipsticked lower lip, Wynona chuckles. "I didn't mean that. I meant this." She gestures at our Easter-colored surroundings. "Checking out the town. Who knew there was such a vibrant local art scene?"

"Me, kind of," I admit. "Yolan mentioned it to me."

"Yolan?" Under her broad black straw hat tied with a red ribbon, Wynona's pale forehead creases in thought. "Wasn't that..."

"Nolan's friend?" I nod. "We talked at the wedding after he introduced us. That was when he first mentioned the tour, although I didn't take him seriously at the time. People make big plans when they're drunk."

"And don't keep them," Wynona agrees.

There's something in the way she eyes me that makes me say, "What?"

A frown. "It's just, about the tour..."

"Don't," I say.

"Fine," she says on a sigh.

Her blue eyes scan down the line of pale yellow, green, and blue storefronts we haven't checked out yet, and her gaze lights up when she stops at one.

Its storefront is crowded with pinup-style dresses, just Wynona's thing.

I take a final bite of crunchy cone and cold ice cream, then rise. "Want to check it out?"

She grins, already rising too.

It takes us one hour, seven dresses, three maybes to decide from, and two bargaining sessions with the pasty gorilla-faced shopkeeper to walk out of there with a label-less plastic bag filled with a not-so-unfamiliar dress.

Wynona gives the bag a rueful little shake. "I can't believe you convinced me to get this."

I catch her hand and guide us along toward the beach. "You looked great in it."

"But one with the exact same teal cartoon cherry print as my bathing suit?" Wynona laughs a little, shaking her glossy dark hair. "Josie is not going to let me live this down."

"You look good in that too," I say neutrally.

But Wynona's already turned eyes with a devilish gleam on me. "Now, if we could just find you a nice matching teal cartoon-cherry tie…"

"Not happening."

Wynona giggles. "C'mon."

I shake my head. "Not going to happen."

She swings my hand up and back. "There's nothing I could do to convince you? Nothing at all?"

I pause, turning an appraising look her way.

"I take it back," she says with a quick giggle.

I shrug, then keep going.

"Where are we going?" she asks.

I pause again just as my stomach rumbles. "You up for some dinner? That ice cream wasn't enough for me."

"Sounds good to me," Wynona says with a smile.

Backtracking our steps isn't hard. There's only one street in this town and only one way we've walked. Locating the coral-colored building with the cool gecko graffiti and delectable burger aromas is easy enough too, although it takes a wait to get the actual burgers and fries.

But when we do get them, just one look—a burger as thick as a cucumber and a carton of fries the size of a laptop—makes 'worth it' more than obvious.

"Guess this is mealtime rush hour," Wynona says ruefully as we pause a few minutes later amid our where-to-sit hunt, seeking out a free bench in vain.

Whether with suntanned teens or laughing locals or bird poo, every new pastel-colored bench we find is full.

I gesture to the further-off beach. "What do you think?"

Wynona's squeezing of my hand is all the answer I need. So we make the transition from hard, slippery cobblestones the size of donuts to smooth bluffs of sand as far as you can crane your neck in either direction.

The breeze has picked up here too, tossing sea smells and cinnamon smells alike like a juggler deciding which ball he likes best.

"We're sitting here?" Wynona has an uncertain note in her voice.

One that's proven right when her sandal-clad foot upturns a rock that was apparently home to several hermit crabs.

At the sight of their advancing clasping claws, I grab Wynona in my arms as she exclaims in fright and hurry us away.

"That would be a no," I say once she's calmed down and I've set her back on her own feet.

Although my arms are still around her.

Most of her bright fuchsia lipstick is still on. I'd like to kiss the rest of it off her.

I'd like to kiss way more than that off her.

Shit, but the food…

I crane my neck one way, then the other. Then I see it, what might work.

"C'mon," I say, taking her hand.

"Do I have much choice?"

Pure Wynona. Sassy. Ironic. A bit pessimistic, but full of humor.

"No," I say, grinning at her and tugging her along.

And she glares at me like she doesn't like it when I take charge.

We trudge over more and more sandy bluffs until we get to it. Hard grey swaths of rock, pocked with the odd hole or dent. Not exactly luxury seating, but…

I scan around the nooks and crannies and dips and swells of the grey hardness until I find it. "Over here."

I stop by the two rocks and gesture to them.

Wynona's already smiling as she sits down on one, her back leaning on the other. "Wow. They're actually really comfortable."

"Good," I say, sitting beside her. "Because this is our seat."

"Sounds like a plan."

We don't dig into the meal—we dig it out. The bun, almost as puffy as cotton candy, seems to have enveloped that crazy-thick burger in doughy stickiness. Meanwhile, the laptop-sized carton seems to have closed its cardboard flaps nearly impenetrably on the fries.

With groans of exasperation, we finally rip everything out and stuff our faces.

A few minutes of good face-stuffing later, Wynona leans further back onto the rock with a blissful look on her face. "This really is good."

I lean back too. "Just good?"

Her face is so pressed-up against my cheek that when she smiles, I can feel her cheek move when her lips pull up.

"Great, maybe," she says.

"Great," I say.

"Great," she says.

"Great," I say, but not to mess with her.

There's something about the word that just occurred to me.

Something familiar, and yet...

Ah.

Yes.

I remember now. "Weird."

"What?" she says.

"What?" I say.

She laughs. "I don't know. You just—you said the word weird."

I turn to shoot her an ironic look. "Now you're going to get on my case for saying the word weird?"

I can see the debate in the flickering of her pupils whether to glare or grin.

She grins. "Yeah."

"Got me," I say. "It just reminded me of something."

"Something," she says, forehead creased. "Oh, my God, something! Of course."

I bop her with the side of my body. "Okay, okay. Just not a happy memory."

"The best ones are."

"What a Wynona thing to say," I quip back.

"Careful." She quirks a black-penciled eyebrow. "We haven't fought today."

"It's just that band—you remember LCD Soundsystem?"

"God, I had a whole summer where I wouldn't turn off 'All My Friends'. Of course I remember! What about them?"

"They had this song, 'Something Great'—"

"Oh, yeah, I remember." She's got on a lazy smile I like. Part of me just wants to kiss her, change the subject entirely. "Another good one."

The silence sits like a hat that's way too big.

She doesn't look at me expectantly, at least.

Shit.

"For months after I ended things with you, I couldn't stop listening to it. Guess you could say it was our breakup song. I even figured out a way to play it on the piano."

Wynona's gaze on me is guarded, thoughtful.

I take her hand. "It's not important. I finally deleted the song off my laptop because I was so sick of it."

Her voice is quiet and not humorous. "Sick of missing me?"

My hand finds hers, and her fingers have formed into a clenched half-fist. I untwine the fingers like a knot. "I guess you could say that."

But they keep tensing up again. "I wish it had been as easy as deleting a song for me."

A glance at her finds her eyes staring off, narrowed at a far-off buoy that can't be the real source of whatever she's feeling.

I close my fingers on hers, tensed and all.

"I drew," she says. "How it felt. Like I had to bury myself and resurrect myself at the same time. Like when most of your personality is shaped by a person, you have to shed it." With her eyes closed, she exhales. "If not, every day is hell. Every day is unbearable. You can't be reminded of them every second of every day. You can't stand it then."

I wrap my arms around her. "I'm sorry you went through that. But you should know it was hard for me too."

"Yes," she says, letting me hold her, her smile sad. "You're sorry I went through that—but not that it happened."

If this is a test, I'll surely fail it.

But I owe Wynona the truth. Nothing less.

"Yes," I say.

"Me too," she says.

Another one of those sad smiles. "At first, I wasn't, of course. I hated it, hated you. Unblocking your Facebook late at night and checking it was like a self-flagellating daily exercise. I wrote so many texts to you that I never sent. But then, somewhere along the way, I realized my life was better for it. In a way, my life was forced onto the right track by it." Sad becomes rueful. "Whether I liked it or not."

"Thank God," I say.

She smiles. "Yeah. I guess so. That's the thing about pain like that—it almost forces you into doing things you normally wouldn't just to get away from it. Remember how long I'd been talking about opening my business, talk, talk, talk, all talk? After, I just did it. Because the fear and the potential pain of what I'd lose if it didn't work out were nothing compared to what I was feeling already. It was like a spur driving me."

"Sounds like you got off easily," I say with almost a chuckle.

She does chuckle. "In some ways."

She exhales, pulling away. Her back is rigid. I can see the delicate pale curves of her spine. Her gaze, when she turns it to me, is resigned.

She smells like the kind of flower I want to devour. Which doesn't make any sense.

"I'm sorry for springing the baby thing on you. I know it's a lot, especially since we just barely re-met. I'm still not sure what I want to do myself. It's only been two weeks. We hardly know each other."

She turns away again, that spine I want to stroke relaxing. She's said what she's going to say. "Don't feel like you have to respond, either. That's all I wanted to say."

"All right," is all I can think to say.

My response would be something between 'I really care about you', 'this is moving way too fast and I don't know why I like it', and 'I'm going to figure out how to make this work'. But I don't say it.

I won't until I know the how and that the when will be soon.

I've already disappointed Wynona once.

The last thing I want is to do it again.

We recline there on the rock-chair while several infinity-sign-shaped clouds with dappled edges float past on their sea of desktop blue sky. By the sea and somewhere unseen, gulls cry. Some swing song plays from afar.

Suddenly, her eyes light up again. "Look!"

I follow her pointing finger to see something moving. A brown-patterned big shell. Four brown and tan speckled legs. A turtle.

"Ooh, look at him go," Wynona exclaims as he makes his way for the sea faster than I'd think a turtle could.

"Wonder where he came from," I say, my gaze already scanning beyond the rocks we're reclining on.

Further down a mostly abandoned beach, twenty or so yards away, I make it out.

Several brown specks on the move, followed by colorful specks.

A few seconds of watching confirms it. It's more turtles making their way to the sea. Only some of these seem to be babies, herded by a group of people.

"Look," I say, nudging Wynona, who watches with a growing smile.

"Maybe volunteers?" she asks. "Let's check it out."

I rise, offering her a hand.

A few minutes later, we find out that yes, those are babies, and yes, those are volunteers helping them to sea. It turns out that they're from the beach on the opposite shore of the island, the one we didn't even know about. The babies, the sunburnt kindly older female volunteer tells us, get confused by the road beside it and the traffic lights and often end up wandering there and getting crushed. It doesn't help that the other beach is so polluted that some of the babies who reach it still don't make it.

"Oh, God, that's horrible," Wynona breathes.

The woman nods her white-bunned head. "That's what we're here for."

Which is how we end up spending the next three hours helping the volunteers transport the turtles from the far beach to this one.

By the end, we're hot, sweaty, exhausted, but wildly happy.

We leave the volunteers with a wave and a smile.

"That was amazing," Wynona says.

"You were amazing," I correct her. "One turtle under each arm."

She chuckles. "Well, they weren't going anywhere, so..."

We head back to the hotel without a word about it. The moon is high in the sky, it's late, and we're tired. There's no need to say what's coming next.

Back in my bed, we make love with a slowness and ease that's fucking amazing.

Everything is until I get the call the next morning.

CHAPTER 21

Wynona

"I should take this," he says, leaving the room.

I don't let the worry worm its way in. I don't let it even form.

No, what we've shared these past few days is bigger than that. It has to be.

I won't live in fear anymore.

In any case, the shaft of sunlight streaming in between the blackout curtains and warming my toes indicates it's another sunny day ahead of us. There's even a tropical bird singing near our window, by the sounds of it.

I let my feet fall on the cool floor and head for the bathroom. By the time I come back out, he's back.

"What was that?" I ask.

"Nothing important," he says.

Something very, very important, his clenched jaw and crossed arms say.

"Emerson," I say softly.

He won't look at me. "It doesn't make any difference to anything."

"Then why not tell me?"

"It's better this way."

His profile, his stance, is a study in indifference. A chosen indifference.

He turns to me and his whole face relaxes. His eyes smile.

His hair is still slick from the shower he just took. I can almost smell his hair from here. Like a beacon back into his arms where everything is safe.

But I can't go there. Not just yet.

"Emerson," I say softly.

"Wynona," he says.

"So, you won't tell me."

"It's not worth telling."

"Then why not?"

His eyes close. He exhales. "Fine. It's just Yolan. He doubled the amount they're going to pay me, shortened the amount of time I'd have to be away. $100,000 for four months. And he'd make me the headliner act."

I blink at him. "What?"

"It's fine, I told him I'm not interested. I've made up my mind, Wyn, and I don't intend to change it."

"But Emerson, you said—"

"The money could come in useful, I'll grant you that," he admits. "Especially with what we now... know. But you can't just jet off for four months, and I won't leave you again. I made that mistake once. Not again."

"And you weren't even going to tell me?" I demand.

"It just would've made things complicated," he growls. "Like it is now."

"It's a good offer," I say. "A damn good one. If you want to be able to do this..."

"I do," he snaps. "But not like this."

"But the exposure too, your career." I eye him steadily. "Emerson, this is the kind of publicity that could put you on the map. That's what you always wanted."

"It is," he admits in a strained voice. "Though not as much as some things."

We stand there, not looking at each other. I need to sit down, but I don't want to move.

Someone once told me it's a power play, silence. You keep your mouth shut, and it makes the person uncomfortable, forces them to speak, even give in. Some people will do a lot to avoid silence.

But this silence only seems to fortify Emerson's decided profile, make it more sure of itself, more hard. More remote.

It only makes the ribbons of doubt in my gut turn into two-hand-thick ropes.

"Emerson," I say quietly. "This is your dream."

"No." He shakes his head in one angry whip. "My dream is making this work."

"But your music... that's your dream too. Making it big. Having lots of people know your work, your songs."

"There are different paths to get there. Maybe it was a childish dream, anyway."

I want to go over there, grab him, and shake him until he listens to me. Until he gives some sign that he's not a statue letting words flow over him as useless as water.

"You said that lucky breaks can come only once in a lifetime," I remind him quietly. "That when they come, you sure as hell had better take them."

He rounds on me with a snarl. "What do you want me to say, Wynona? That I wouldn't take this opportunity anyway? Well, I would. I'd take this opportunity in a second if I hadn't met up with you again. But I did. And that's it. It changes everything."

Tears cloud my eyes, my voice too. "I can't have you give this up for me. This means too much to you."

His gaze avoids mine. "And yet, there are things that mean more to me."

"Emerson—"

"Wynona." The denim blues of his eyes, when he finally turns them on me, are tortured, almost beseeching. "Don't make this any harder on me than it has to be."

"But—"

"You think I'd leave you now that I know... that?" He gestures at my belly. "God, no. Over my dead body."

It's that tone that does it, that makes my next words—We can't even talk about it?—die in my throat.

"So, that's it then?" I say in a wooden voice.

"That's it, then," Emerson says before he stalks out of the room.

And that is it.

We avoid each other for the next few hours. When I head out for some much-needed air and get a tap on the shoulder, I jump, though it's only Josie.

"How are you not in a better mood?" she demands, looking me up and down. "Most men would go running and screaming if you so much as coughed the word 'baby', let alone were pregnant with theirs."

"I know," I say. "And his reaction has been great, thoughtful, though we haven't talked specifics. But there's something else."

"His crazy ex is back?" Josie asks, starting to walk along the beach.

"No," I say, walking alongside her.

"He wants to live on the island forever?"

"No," I say.

"Well, what is it, then?"

"I would tell you if you'd give me a chance to speak!" I grumble.

"Sorry," Josie says with a sigh. "I was just talking to Mom a few minutes ago. She's been looking after my plants, and I just found out that my calathea finally bit the dust. It was a long time coming, but still. Death hurts." Her voice takes on a more musing tone. "Must suck to be God. Whoops! You were saying?"

"I'm sorry about your calathea," I say patiently. "But it's just... remember that offer to go on tour I told you Emerson got?"

"Yeah, that he gave up for you?"

"That's the one." I sit down on a bench. Talking about stressful things has a way of tiring me out more than actual exercise. "Well, the man in charge just doubled how much he's offering Emerson to come and offered him the top act."

"Damn," Josie says, sitting beside me.

"Damn is right." I sigh. "This is a once-in-a-lifetime opportunity, and you know what he's doing?"

"He's giving it up," Josie murmurs.

"Yep." I groan. "On account of yours truly. If he doesn't hate me in a week or a month, he's sure to in a few more years."

"But if you encourage him..."

"I have been!" I say. "I don't know how things would work or if they even would, but I can't have him give this up on account of me. Not in good conscience."

"But at the end of the day, it is his decision," Josie says softly.

I snort. "And he's making the wrong one. I can't let him do that."

A pause as Josie eyes me steadily. "What are you going to do?"

I sit up, then flop back down on the bench again. "I don't know."

"Well, if I remember correctly, Emerson's as stubborn as all the other Storm boys," Josie says ruefully. "So, you have your work cut out for you."

"I know."

"And are you sure you even want to do this? I mean, the man is basically treating you like a queen, with all signs that treatment will continue once you get home. This was your first love, Wynona."

"My only love," I correct her. "But here's the thing. Sometimes if you love someone, you have to do what's best for them instead of what's best for you. Even if they don't want you to."

A pause, then Josie's suspicious voice. "Have you finally started secretly reading those self-help books I gave you?"

I roll my eyes. "Nope. Just something I learned from my sister, you could say."

"You mean what I told you about what Emerson did when he… ah. Oh. Well."

"I owe it to him," I say. "He did the same for me. He did what was best for me, even when I didn't want him to."

"Well," Josie says after a pause.

A longer pause.

"That's it?" I say.

"That's it," she says. "I'm not sure there's any point in arguing with you."

"Because I'm right?"

"Because I don't know," she says before exhaling. "You know you're risking a lot if you stand your ground on this, don't you?"

"I risk a lot anyway," I say softly. "Anyway, Jos. Remember that woo-woo thing I told you was stupid a few years back when you tried advising me to use it?"

Josie's voice is very unimpressed. "You mean intuition?"

"Yeah, that. Well, I'm having a kick from it. Like the gods are giving me a nudge or something. So, I'm going to go for it."

"Well." Josie chuckles. "I'm not going to argue with that."

I chuckle too. "Good. Anyway, when I get back, I'll go talk some sense into Emerson. You'll see."

Josie just lifts her eyebrows and smiles.

Talking some sense into Emerson does not go at all how I'd like.

Maybe I should've given it more time. Maybe I should've written a draft of my reasons and what I was going to do beforehand like I did sometimes for tricky conversations with long-term clients—like one who, for unknown reasons, was one hundred percent dead-set on getting a penis tattooed onto his face. Maybe I should've waited for that elusive perfect time and place that doesn't seem to exist outside of movie studios and mood lighting.

We're cuddling in bed and so cozy, and everything is so very nice, that I have to. I have to settle it so I can enjoy myself fully.

That's another major difference between Josie and me, always has been. When there's something I'm dreading to do, something I'm putting off, I carry it with me.

"Emerson," I say, "I know you don't want to talk about the tour, but I want you to go."

His whole body stiffens. "I'm not going. End of discussion."

I sit up straight. "I can't let you do this. I'd never forgive myself."

His white teeth are clenched, his blue eyes fiery. "And I'd never forgive myself if I left you now, of all times."

His words travel straight through me, just about rub my heart.

God, I could kiss him for saying something a lot less sweet than that.

But right now, it's not time for feeling touched and going soft. I can't let this just drop.

"By the time you come back, I'll still have a few more months before I give birth, and—"

"It's not just about that." He scowls.

"What is it about, then?" I ask.

He shakes his head. "Not going to say it again."

I take his hand. "Hey, I'm not the same person I was then. I've got a great job, friends, a life of my own. I won't fall apart when you're gone."

But Emerson just lets me hold his hand, doesn't hold it back. He looks at me hard. "Don't you see, though, that there will always be something else? If this goes well, there will be another, bigger tour after this that will pay five times as much and have me performing for the Queen. If we start going down this road, this road where I choose music over you, there may be no going back."

His powerful shoulders tense as he shakes his head. "Momentum's like that. Once you have it, you'd be a fool to throw it away. A tour like this, and what comes after, it could last years, half a decade. I'm not willing to spend that or anywhere near that away from you."

I squeeze his hand, but it's as rigid as a chair leg. "Then just take this tour and swear off anything else."

"It's not that easy," he says.

When I don't answer, he adds, "That's what happened to my parents."

I don't say a word. I hardly breathe. Emerson never liked to talk about it. But now…

"They were crazy in love too," he says. "Held hands everywhere, and my dad treated her like a queen. But he had to go away for work, and Mom hated traveling, so they'd be apart for a few weeks at a time. Unless a deal went sour and Dad had to do damage control and stay a month or two. And then his trips started lasting months at a time. That's when he started cheating on her, during those long spans apart. It didn't make it right, what he did. But they were fine until they decided to try doing long-distance long-term." His steady gaze meets mine. "They were fine until they decided to put work over their relationship."

I glare right back at him. "What are you saying, that if we go long-distance now, you'll end up cheating on me?"

"No, hell no," he says, scowling even deeper. "Just that's it's an added stress. A really fucking big one."

Seeing the firm lines of his face now, I realize it. That my bringing it up again has only dug Emerson's feet in deeper.

Shit.

When I move my face close to him, my voice comes out a whisper. "You made a sacrifice for me once. Why can't you let me do the same for you?"

His gaze wavers. He closes his eyes and exhales.

Finally, he turns away. "Because you wouldn't be better off for it this time. I'm not willing to risk what we have. Not again."

His back to me, he says, "And that's final," to the wall.

I sit there. I wait.

For what, I'm not sure, only it's not for him to lie down without another word.

It's not for me to stare into the dark, wondering what the hell I'm going to do now.

It takes a few minutes for it to hit me.

That it really is final.

I lie down. Pull the sheet up to my shoulder. Close my eyes as if I were going to sleep.

But I don't go to sleep.

The quiet is just blank space for my mind to talk over.

My mind has words—oh, it has words.

Like, You can't let this happen. You know this isn't right.

Round and round and round they go, everything I should've said—No, what I said is final, I won't let you give this up for me, everything I should've done—left for emphasis, looked into leaving tomorrow, and his probable reactions—frustration, incredulity, maybe even rage.

I lie here thinking of all the things I should've said and done. All the things it's too late to say and do.

He said it himself—that's final.

I saw it, too, the finality written on every part of Emerson's face.

Worst of all, I know it.

There'd be no point staying the rest of the week here at the resort with him.

I won't get through to him. Nothing will.

If I want to do the right thing, make the right choice, I'll have to do it alone.

And I'll have to do it now.

My knees tense.

Somewhere amid the battle royale between what I should do, leave, and what I want to do, stay, I fall asleep.

I wake up to the soft sound of music. So soft, I normally would've slept right through it.

I peek one eye open.

It's dark. There's a silhouette through the clear glass of the closed sliding door.

It's him.

He's inclined on a hammock, the moonlight casting his features into semi-visibility. He's got his keyboard in his lap, and he's playing.

I strain to hear, to join the notes to a song I've heard before, but I can't.

It's a new song, a beautiful song.

And one glance at his face and it's obvious. He's loving every minute of it.

That is what focus looks like. Joy.

That is what he's giving up for me.

I can't let him.

I close my eyes against the tears. If only I could close them against this… this decision I have to make.

Sometimes, love means doing what they won't for themselves. Doing things that will hurt you, hurt them.

I can't take that away from him. Not for all the safety and security in the world.

And so, I lie there as the tears escape my closed eyelids as if my decision hasn't been made for me. As if, by sleeping, somehow, this will all get better.

Next time I wake up, there's a warmth, a safety in me that knows he's right there beside me.

It's insidious, this warmth. Like a blanket muffling what I need to do.

I know that if I let myself ease into it, let myself wrap my arms around him, even let myself doze off, it's over.

This is my last chance.

The decision comes to me with a swift clarity, like the air after a good rain. I have to go now.

I can't wait, can't put it off, can't even think it over a second longer.

It's clear as day how the days after today will unroll if I let them. Tomorrow, I will still hold it close, this 'should' of mine. I'll try to ease him into considering it. I'll try to cradle it and turn it over in my mind, this idea I have now.

It won't work.

Emerson won't so much as glance its way. His heels will dig in deep as roots. The hours will tug at the loose threads of my idea, all the ways it won't work, all the ways I can't do it.

Which is why I have to do it now. Right now.

Before I get the sleep I think will give me strength but will only give me fear.

So, I do it.

I get out of the bed as quietly as I can. I go back to my room. And then I get my things. I wake up Josie, and she agrees with what I tell her I have to do. She insists on coming along.

And then we've called the taxi to the airport and it's done.

As simple as that.

On the taxi ride to the airport, with the night sky outside studded with stars, I lean forward to tell the taxi driver to turn around half a dozen times. My finger is so close to Emerson's name on my phone that I'm surprised I don't accidentally press it.

And yet, somehow, we get there. There's a flight leaving in an hour and a half with seats still left. We buy ourselves tickets.

That hour and a half blurs past like a dream. Like maybe I never really got out of bed, just rolled onto the other side of the pillow and dozed back off.

It's so easy, so quick. Getting our tickets, passing through security and the gates. As if it's a game. As if I'm traveling to a different dimension. Or maybe away from one.

Uncanny, how it feels as though I'm getting both further away and closer to myself. Further away from the Wynona who was weak and trapped in love. Closer to the one who takes the right action like a judge's mallet falling, fast and final.

I keep my phone on airplane mode even when I get off the plane.

CHAPTER 22

Emerson

I wake up angry, relieved.

We argued, and yet, she's still here, we can still…

I roll over to look at the empty space in the bed next to me. It still bears her imprint in the wrinkles and dip of the white silk sheets.

Her imprint—but not her.

A glance around confirms it. She's not here.

The bathroom door's open.

She must've gone back to her room.

And yet…

I've never bought into 'gut feelings'. But right now, mine's just about kicking me.

I throw on a pair of pink and silver Bermuda shorts Nolan gave me as a joke, then head down the hallway to her room.

Her door is open. It takes all of two seconds to see that she's not inside.

A four-foot-nothing cleaning woman blinks at me in the middle of spraying down the mirror.

"She's gone?" I say.

She blinks at me again and smiles with a nod.

Fuck. She wouldn't have.

I storm to the front desk.

"The woman in Room 204?" I ask the concierge.

"She checked out, sir," he replies. "Said she had a plane to catch."

Fuck no.

I wheel around and storm back to my room.

That's when I think to check my phone.

I chuckle darkly, a snarl twisting my features as I see what she's left me.

All she's left me.

And there it is. I'm sorry, Emerson. But this is the right thing to do.

My legs sit me down on the bed as I read and reread it. As if there were another meaning other than the one staring me right in the fucking face.

It's too early to hear anything other than the bang of furious half-formed thoughts in my head. How could she? Why would... how did this... what am I... ?

Everything falls flat against the one certainty. I have to go after her.

Lounge around here while she's probably on a plane home right this second?

Fuck that.

If I stayed here another day, another hour, then every place I went, every activity I did, would only remind me of her.

Trying to call her up only goes straight to voicemail, of course.

For the next few hours, I go through the motions. I hit up Jeremy, who offers his sympathy and to come along, but I can see he wants to stay. I let him. I pack up my things. Check out at the lobby with the startled concierge. Catch a cab. Navigate through the swarming airport. Argue with a ticket attendant until I get a ticket on the next flight. Catch a few hours of rest on the airport bench. Get on the flight. Sleep some more. Pay for Wi-Fi so I can send her an email. Pass out again. Check my email—no response.

Arrive. Get a cab. Get back to my place. Call her up again.

This time, it rings, but she doesn't answer. I stalk to my car, shove my key in the ignition, and… freeze.

Fuck.

It's eleven PM, but that's not what's stopping me.

It's that I don't know Wynona's fucking address.

I lean back in the car seat and close my eyes.

Think…

I call the next number that comes into my head. The only one I can think of, at this point.

"Hello, stranger," Nolan says jovially. "Boy, do I have some tales for you."

"Hey," I say, trying not to sound too shitty. "How was the honeymoon?"

I want to see Wynona now. But there's no point in being a complete dick to my brother.

"Glorious, just glorious," he says, in a good enough mood for the both of us. "Did you know that Bangkok has the longest name of any city in the world? You know what the full version is?"

"Something tells me you're going to tell me," I say wryly.

"It's Krung Thep Mahanakhon Amon Rattanakosin Mahinthara Ayuthaya Mahadilok Phop Noppharat Ratchathani Burirom Udomratchaniwet Mahasathan Amon Piman Awatan Sathit Sakkathattiya Witsanukam Prasit," he says, cracking up. "It's like a different world over there, let me tell you. The national anthem is played publicly twice a day. And these people, they know respect, man. Doesn't matter if you're in a train station, mall, or busy market, everyone, even the freaking monkeys, will stop moving and bow respectfully when the song ends. Can you believe it?"

"Shit," I say.

"Yeah, shit," Nolan says musingly. "What's up with you? How goes paradise?"

"Can you ask Sierra for Wynona's address?"

"Sure, I'll just…" Nolan pauses. "Hold on. Why do you need her address?"

"We had an argument," I admit. "Now she won't return my calls, won't even let me explain. We both flew back. I'm in New York now."

"Ooh," he says.

"Damn," he says.

"Hmm," he says.

"Are you going to ask her or not?" I growl.

"Fine, fine." His hands are up, if I know my brother at all well. "Don't shoot the messenger."

The sound of muffled voices, then Nolan says, "Sierra wants to know why."

"Then tell her why," I find myself growling.

More muffled voices, then, "She doesn't think she should tell you."

"Great," I growl.

"What's going on?" Nolan says. "I thought you guys were capital-G good."

"Yolan, that guy you hooked me up with? He gave me a great offer to go on tour."

"And the problem with that is?"

"I'm not going to take it."

Nolan snorts. "Did you bump your head on a beach rock or something?"

"No. Wynona and I couldn't do long-distance last time. I'm not about to make the same mistake again."

"Huh." I can almost hear Nolan scratching his head. "So, what's the problem then?"

I consider mentioning the baby—in all the chaos of these past twelve hours I'd all but forgotten—but ultimately decide against it. I will tell my brothers about it, but not yet.

"The problem is that Wynona thinks I should take the opportunity," I tell him. "She's so dead-set on it that she won't take no for an answer."

"Oh, hmm," Nolan says. "That is a problem."

"She left without a word to me," I say. "I woke up and found her gone."

"Oh," Nolan says. "Sounds serious."

"Yeah."

Silence.

"You really like her, don't you?" he asks, amused. "As much as you like that shoe composer guy."

"You mean Schumann," I say drily. "And almost."

A low, long whistle. "Damn. You really like her, don't you?"

"Do we have to get into it?"

Nolan chuckles. "Boy, do you have it bad. I guessed as much. The rest of us have been finding our ladies, oldest to youngest. It was your turn."

"Glad I'm meeting the timeline."

"You know that's not what I meant."

"Yeah, yeah."

I listen to the silence and wonder what Nolan's going to fill it with this time.

That's my brother for you, jokester, talker. Greyson was always the serious one, the one who could sort things out even when you didn't know they needed to be. Landon could always lay out things with logic that you never expected. And me, I could play piano.

"Listen, I am sorry," Nolan says.

"It's okay," I say. "Sierra's being loyal to her friend. I get it. I'll find another way."

"I'm not sorry about that," he says.

"Okay?"

He chuckles. "If you really like this woman, then man, are you in for a world of pain."

"Is that supposed to make me feel better?"

"Nah, that's supposed to warn you. If you really think you want this, you'd better think it over nice and long. Because love, real love, not lust or a nice thing for now—real, actual, honest-to-God love, it'll rip you apart, and when it puts you back together, you very well may not like what's left."

"Dude."

"Don't dude me." I have the rare sense, as acute as a knock on my funny bone, that Nolan is being dead serious for once. "You were with this girl before. You never let us meet her, but I was there for the aftermath. She tore you up good, man."

"Nolan, I don't need—"

"But that's just it," he snaps. "I think you do need to hear this. Listen to me, Emerson, and listen to me carefully. If you love this girl, if you really, truly love her and if you're ready to fight like hell for her, you have to know what it means. What it could mean. I've been there—hell, I am there. In the movies and books, the end scene, the happily ever after, is the couple riding off into the sunset, in love, feeling so complete and easy. It's a fucking joke." His voice becomes harsh. "I don't say this to knock Sierra. That woman is the best thing that's ever happened to me, hands down. But what I've got with her, it's kicked my ass. Stripped me bare. At the risk of sounding like a complete ass, I'll admit it. I've had times when I wanted nothing more than to run as far as I could away from this, from her. Not because I didn't love her but because I did." He almost chuckles. "Because that woman will be the near-death of me. She challenges me, terrifies me. Because that's what love is—a teeter-totter where you're both always fucking moving and sometimes, there's a wind. Other times, a goddamn tornado. You ready for that?"

"I..." To say that I hadn't expected this out of Nolan would be a huge understatement. I can't remember the last time he said this many serious words in a sentence, let alone several sentences strung together. "I don't know."

"Not good enough," he says. "You'd better not go to her until you do. Because you'll be doing both of you a big fucking disservice."

"I know I want to be with her. That's not enough?"

"Not unless you accept that it will be hard. Not always, maybe even not soon, though it sounds like it. Otherwise, what's the point?"

"I don't know about that," I say. "Relationships can be a success, even if they end early. As long as you learn things."

"I don't disagree," Nolan says neutrally. "Here's what I don't joke about in any of my shows because it's too damn sad, and this world is sad enough already. We're a people distracted to distraction. Most of us can hardly read a book, let alone concentrate on a conversation we're in. Commitment isn't trendy these days. We lazily change our minds at the slightest good argument. We secretly wish for other lives, other partners at the first glimpse of something better. We don't have God or morality or even tradition telling us what to do anymore, so we don't stick with it. We like the new and we like the exciting. We've seen the flipside of too much commitment, and it's so ugly and hideous and haunting, a life wasted with a slow noose of a partner, that we've thrown ourselves at the opposite."

"What are you getting at?" I snap.

This is both typical and atypical. Nolan has a thing for ranting on the abstract, debating on both sides. But almost never seriously. Why is he taking this so seriously?

"What I'm getting at here, Emerson," he continues, "is that before you go chasing Wynona down, you'd better make damn sure this is what you want, for good. Otherwise, you're putting you both in a world of pain."

"Dude."

"What?"

"We were at the beach resort for two weeks. I can't have a bit more time to figure out where this is going?"

"I thought you knew you wanted to be with her."

"I do, but... you're talking like I need to know the end of this already when we've both barely just started."

"Right now, it's an easy transition point," Nolan says, "an easy break from a paradise world to the real one. She's given you an easy out, little brother. I'd make sure that you don't want to take it. I mean, you gave her up once."

"I only did that for her own good."

Nolan makes a skeptical noise. "And what about after that?"

"After that, I... I felt ashamed, okay? I didn't want to reach out too soon and derail everything she'd accomplished, how far she'd gotten, and then, even later, I saw how well she was doing and I tried to reach out, and when she wouldn't go for it, you know what, I recognized that I deserved it. Expecting her to get her shit together and wait years for me, what was that? What was I thinking?"

Silence.

Hell, this is not the conversation I expected to be having when I called my brother up.

I can't tell if the sudden hit of weariness is from it or my recent flight.

"Nolan?" I ask.

"Yeah?"

"What made it click for you? You never had many serious girlfriends, you never even believed in marriage, and then..."

"And then, Sierra," he says. "What made it click for me was that I stayed. That when it got so hard I usually would've fucked off, given up, I stayed. I wanted to stay more than I wanted to leave. And she stayed too."

"That's it?"

A chuckle. "Of course that's not it. She's an amazing woman. I lucked out finding her. But don't get me wrong. I could've screwed it up. But it came to a point when I realized something. I could've run from her, run to the next woman who didn't know my bullshit and didn't get pissed off at it. But I wouldn't be running from her, from Sierra. I'd be running from myself. From seeing myself reflected in her eyes." An exhale that almost turns into a chuckle. Almost. "And you know what? Sometimes, I fucking hate it, how she will call me out. How she doesn't let me get away with a lot of my tricks. But most of the time, I like it. I don't have to pretend anymore, Emerson."

This silence is the same that's in my head.

"Dude," I say.

"I know, I know," he says.

"How... where did this come from?"

"I took an ayahuasca trip," he admits. "Greyson had me down in Peru with this shaman. It was pretty cool. Other than that... I'd say it came from her."

"Hey, you remember those parties we used to go to?" he asks in that same musing voice. Clearly, I've got him in a mood. Not that I mind. The way we're talking about the real stuff, it almost reminds me of her. Wynona. "At the Watson mansion?"

"Hell, we were what, early twenties, late teens?" I laugh. "God, those were the days."

I can almost see it now.

A six-story beachfront villa house. Strategically placed purple, pink, and blue lights painting everyone. Enough loud house music that the aliens were probably grooving somewhere.

I DJed there once or twice.

They went on for a good year or two, the Watson parties, until their parents divorced.

"At first, those parties were amazing," Nolan's saying. "An open bar with every pricey liquor you could think of. Those acrobats and jugglers with fire. That sauna full of the most gorgeous naked women you'd see anywhere. But I don't know, maybe it was the fourth or fifth time you were there, didn't it start to feel a bit…"

"Empty," I say, frowning. "Yeah."

His words scrape at me.

He lets the silence sit.

Fuck, this is not what I need to be thinking about right now.

What I need to figure out is how to get her back.

"I really should get going," I tell him.

"Yeah, yeah," he says. "Sorry for going off on a bit of a tangent. Just wanted to make sure that you knew what you were getting into."

"Thanks," I say. "I think."

He chuckles. "Oh, and Wynona's address is 314 Clair Creek Blvd."

"Wait, what?"

"Sierra wrote it down while we were talking. Guess all my deep mumbo-jumbo convinced her."

"Shit, thanks." 314 Clair Creek Blvd. 314…

"All right. Good luck, then. Maybe you should leave it until tomorrow."

Now I'm the one chuckling. "Not a chance. Wynona's a night owl. She'll be up. And she'll want to see me."

"You're so sure?"

"I am."

"Why?"

"Because I know. I don't care what you said. I've felt it myself. How it's shit sometimes, love. How it tears at you. How in a lot of ways, it's easier with the others, the ones you care less about. But I want her. The good, the bad, all of it. I want to be with her, man."

Nolan laughs and keeps on laughing. "All right, all right. I'll leave you to it, then."

Next thing I know, I've plugged the address into my GPS, am heading there.

As I drive, every so often, the moon peers out of its clouds like an eye glimpsing me every so often.

I pass a lot of things once I get into the neighborhoods. I pass a series of trashcans painted like different tropical red and yellow and green and brown and scarlet and black and ochre and peach birds that I'm pretty sure don't exist. I pass a homeless man who looks like a bit like my dad, if my dad had ever decided to be homeless and stick a cigarette in the hole of a missing tooth.

My air conditioner is blasting goosebumps up and down my arms. Maybe it's nervousness.

Fuck, I don't want to do this.

In the same way you don't want to check your mark for the big test but have to, want to. Only you can't stand the looming outcome.

I pass some teens doing pushups. It seems too late for all this. For the number of people on the streets. But it's the first real summer night we've had, maybe. Maybe it's like hope is in the air.

Or maybe it's me.

Fuck, I'm getting sentimental.

Guess Nolan really got to me.

Or this girl. This girl who is so much more than that.

This girl who's like, well…

Like a smile out of nowhere.

Wynona.

I smile, thinking of how she got pissed when she thought about the boring meaning of her name—firstborn daughter.

"Firstborn daughter?" she groaned, years ago, one time when we were hanging out, bored, and were talking about just about everything. "What the hell is all that about?"

I wish I'd told her.

I probably wouldn't now.

It sounds silly, thinking it. Even in my head, it sounds like a fucking poem.

That she, Wynona Cowell, can't be described with just a name, or a word, or a string of them. That throwing some meaning from some name on her would just pigeonhole her, try to categorize what can't be categorized.

Because she's every word and its reverse.

And just when you think you know her, she throws you for a loop.

And when it comes to her, I don't have the slightest fucking clue what I'll find when I get to her.

Maybe it won't be good—probably.

But to know Wynona is to know that you have to try.

And all at once, I'm there. It's a relief.

These thoughts I'm having, they don't feel like mine. They feel too lyrical, like some author's tossed a few phrases into my head to make the story beat flow.

But what the hell do I know?

Her place is a chic glass condo building between a pizza shop and a sandwich restaurant. 314 Clair Creek Blvd.

I go in and stare at the intercom. I scroll down until I get to her name. I press in the numbers on the dial pad. I wait.

I didn't bring anything for her, I realize. No peace-treaty gift. No nothing.

She doesn't answer.

There's mud on my shoes, still, from the trip. And I never noticed.

I dial the numbers again, call her phone too. She picks up.

"Emerson. I don't want to—"

"Just hear me out. Then I'll leave you alone."

She tries to out-silence me, one second... two seconds... three... four... loses.

"Fine," she says. "I'll come down."

She comes down, nods to me, walks on past.

"Where are we going?" I ask.

"I know a place," she says.

Her nearness, her coolness. She's wearing red and black velour sweats, and of course, her ass looks great.

My cock flexes.

She doesn't so much as look over her shoulder.

I don't so much as try to keep pace.

Her place is a bench on a patch of grass that apparently exists only for dogs to do their business. She sits down on the far left. I sit down on the far right.

"You just left," I say.

"I had to," she says. "I'm sorry."

"You didn't."

"I did."

"You don't understand." She's talking to her swinging red-lace Doc Martens. Didn't realize I missed them until I saw her, here and now. "I had to do it then, otherwise I wouldn't have."

"Even better."

Her head jolts so she can fix me with those frustrated blue eyes. They look softer without their usual black shadow, more fragile somehow. "No. It wouldn't be. I stand by what I said. I won't have you stay here and miss out on the tour on account of me."

"And I won't go," I return easily.

She turns away. "I can't do this. Not unless you go."

I find myself on my feet. I can't sit and say this, deal with this. "C'mon. Really? You're going to blackmail me into going? Go or we're through, is that it?"

She turns to look at me sadly, like I've gotten the completely wrong answer on the test I didn't know I was taking. "No, Emerson."

"Then what?" I almost laugh with exasperation. "What the hell is it, then?"

She rises too and speaks to a point between me and her. "You know I'm right."

"No," I say. "The only thing I know is that I want to be with you."

Her eyes flicker to me, a half-answered question in them. "Even if... even if it means waiting?"

"Not like that."

She turns away. "I think we both know. That's the solution. We separate for a time, while you do this contract. And then, when you come back—"

"You can't be serious," I say hollowly.

She speaks to the ground, the cracked sidewalk beside the sparse patch of grass. "I don't see any other way. Do you?"

"I see every other way but that."

She frowns. "If we can't get through this, then what's the point?"

"What are you saying?" I take a step toward her. "Jesus, Wyn. You're carrying my child, our child—"

"Don't," she whimpers, turning away. "Just please listen to me, Emerson. If we can't do a few months apart, then what's the point? It's not like this is a long-term arrangement. You go, do the tour, then you come back. Being a couple is full of difficult situations. If we can't overcome this most basic one, then what's the point?"

My hand clenches on the back on the bench like it's to blame. "But you're saying that we aren't doing this as a couple. Isn't that what you're saying?"

"Wouldn't that be for the best?" she asks. "I'm not saying I'll date other people or that I want you to. Just… your whole fear is repeating what happened again. So, we won't have to check in every day, or even every few days."

As I watch her, it gradually dawns on me.

She's serious.

Just as serious as I was before. She's willing to risk everything.

To have everything… maybe.

"Fine." The coolness of my voice surprises me, almost like a curtain drawing over something I hadn't even realized was open. "You want out, you've got it. I'm done with fighting for this, Wynona. I'll go on tour. And when I'm back… we'll see."

I'm walking away before she answers so I won't wait for it, search for it in her eyes.

"We'll see," she says softly behind me, like it was a question.

CHAPTER 23

Wynona

We'll see...

I'm an idiot.

The kind of idiot who sits on a sketchy park bench at midnight alone. The kind who cries for what's completely her fault, what was entirely avoidable. Who cries and cries and cries and can't stop.

Like an idiot. Like a stupid baby.

He's gone now, so I can't explain it to him. How being strong and making the right decision when it's hard, especially when it's hard, is a kind of addiction. How once you get momentum, the scariest thing is losing it.

How one day soon, I hope he'll thank me. I hope he'll wait for me. Wait for us.

I sit on the cool park bench under the murky moonlight. The traffic noises are all far away, like even they don't want anything to do with me.

Maybe this is a kind of cowardice, ending things before he can. Doing it on my own terms.

Maybe.

Probably.

But I saw him that night, and I've seen him countless other ones. Other nights when he's played, whether it's just for me or in front of people, and that look in his eyes like he's too lucky for words.

He's never really talked about it, but he doesn't have to.

It's joy. Plain and simple. Pure and unadulterated.

This—playing music—is Emerson's dream, and going on tour is part of it.

And I won't take that away from him. Whatever the cost.

I get up and start walking home. I try not to search the streets for him coming back, to fight for us one more time. Even though he's done it enough. Even though I shouldn't.

But there's no one there. He's not coming back.

And I don't blame him.

I go back to my apartment, pat my dogs, and go to bed.

My tears are polite. They wait until all my makeup's off, and I'm tucked in bed, with my dogs snuggled in beside me, to come and take over. And then, I keep turning to the other side of the pillow to find they've conquered it, and it's wet already.

**

The next week is one day. I schedule every client I can.

There's a solace in it, losing myself in my art. Getting the curve of a wolf tattoo just right. Seeing the image in my head sketched onto an arm, a bicep, a leg, a lower back.

A person going away the same, but not quite. Making their body into art, a monument, a memory.

Expressing something.

About tattoos, I always hear people say, "I don't have anything that I like enough to be sure that I'd want it there for so long," and I get that. I've thought it myself.

And yet, we are given these bodies with no choice. Some parts we like, others not so much. And yet, by and large, we stick with these parts, whether or not we are sure we want them there for so long.

So I have a sort of respect for the wild ones, the ones who say 'what the hell' and stick out an arm, a leg, a neck. Get something imprinted there that lasts.

Our bodies change as we age, there's no choice in that. Taut skin sags. Hair thins and goes silver, then white. Bad posture catches up with us and wins. But I'd like to think that even though they fade, these colors I etch into people's bodies, it's a bit different.

It's one of the few things we can and do choose about these skin sacks we walk around in.

Then again, I'm biased. I have to be.

I'm a tattoo artist. I've got a few myself.

**

The seventh night of the seventh day I've been back, I'm at my place with Josie and Sierra, just like old times.

"So, tell us," Josie says after Sierra's passed her the Moose Tracks Tom and Jerry's, "the insider scoop on marriage."

"Oh." Sierra tosses her red-brown hair with an impish smile. "So, all those dark, terrible things that Nolan wouldn't want me to tell you?"

"Definitely," I confirm.

"Well... he does leave his dirty socks on the floor sometimes," she recounts, eyes narrowed in faux thought. "But that's nothing compared to the satanic rituals he does every full moon."

We crack up, and Josie elbows her, her mouth full of ice cream. "Jerk."

"No, honestly, it's great," Sierra says. "Not all rainbows and roses. And we fight, like all couples. But I'm happy. Though yeah, it's a bit of a mindfuck."

"Now we're getting somewhere," Josie says happily. "Do tell."

"Well, just... when you're married, it's so... permanent. Like you're really doing this. Like when he's annoying or a bit of a grumpy jerk, you're like, 'Shit, I really signed up for this f-o-r-e-v-e-r?'"

"And?" Josie says, leaning in, her coral lips drawn back in amused horror.

Sierra sighs. "The answer is yes, and yes, I don't regret it. Not too, too much, at least."

We all giggle about that.

"Wasn't this a movie night?" I ask as their gazes swing my way.

Maybe I'm being paranoid, but I feel like I can almost see the questions about Emerson forming in their heads. And I both want to and don't want to talk about it. So, there you go.

"No," Josie says in a scolding tone. "This was movie and onesie night, hello?"

She points to her hilariously oversized narwhal onesie and I can't help it. I crack up.

At that, Sierra flips up the hood of hers, a giant polka-dot octopus, and I flip up mine, a cow. We laugh and laugh.

"Remember that time we went clubbing in these?" Josie recalls, leaning on the side of the couch, giggling at the thought.

"How that bouncer almost wouldn't let us in?" Sierra says. "How we had to dance so crazily and cause such a ruckus outside that he ushered us in just to get rid of us?"

"I'm surprised he didn't just boot us," I say, chuckling myself.

"Oh, no, he had a crush on Josie," Sierra recalls, her eyebrows jumping as she glances at her. "Didn't you go on a few dates with him afterward?"

"Yes," Josie says with a sigh. "But alas, he had a toe fetish."

We lose it over that.

Then, on comes Clueless, and I go grab everyone some popcorn.

After pausing the movie so Sierra can go to the bathroom, I call Josie over to show her an event on Facebook. It's a fun outdoor dance party in the woods, and she's impressed.

But after that, she looks at me carefully and says, "I saw something about Emerson. About the concert he's in. Do you..."

"Sure." The carefree voice I use isn't mine, doesn't feel how I feel. It's the one I've taken on to deal with this whole thing.

So, she types something in on Google and up comes the article in The New York Times.

Top Classical Concert Showcases Young Talent, the headline reads. And, the first picture of the article, there he is.

Wearing that face, that so-into-it handsome face that convinced me I had to let him go. My gaze is so intent on him that for the first few seconds, I don't notice.

But then I do.

She's standing too close to the piano. She's too pretty. She's singing along with Emerson's playing, but that doesn't seem to matter.

What does is how she's looking at him.

"Oh, God..."

The words slip out before I can stop them. And suddenly, the voice is gone and every lie I could tell.

It seems ridiculous. Why would I even want to?

Maybe because as tears come to my eyes, I remember that talking about it makes it more real, makes it worse.

Even if it's true. Of course it's true.

"Wyn?" Sierra says hesitantly, back from the bathroom.

"I'm sorry." Josie quickly clicks away. "I shouldn't have shown you that. I should've—"

"No," I say. "It's fine. I can't just avoid it."

"Maybe you should," Sierra says quietly. "Though, if you want to talk about it…"

"I feel like a fool," I say. "I was the one who convinced him to go, was dead-set on him going. And guys, I'm freaking pregnant."

Their arms wrap around me, and I remember why I wanted to tell them. These girls, these women, they know the depths of me, and almost miraculously, they still like me. They're my best friends.

Sure, a few times, they've been bitches, and that time in high school with that Irish boy made me seriously consider switching out Josie's eyebrow cream for Nair, but I love them.

"It's just a picture," Josie says. "And if Emerson really cares for you that much…"

"He wanted to stay together while he was gone." The words come out wooden and accusing. The picture is branded into my mind. "I was the one who said no."

"Hey, listen to me," Sierra says, holding out a scolding finger. "If this man is your man, some classical music bitch isn't going to take that away. If he's your guy, then he's not going to be swayed from that."

"But Sierra, four months away when I was the one who insisted—"

"Hey," she says, finger pressing into my chest. "End of."

"She's right," Josie says. "Listen to the married lady."

Sierra snorts. "I don't claim to be some relationship guru, but let me tell you this. Out of all the guys I dated, with all the times it didn't work out, I started thinking it was me. Maybe I had too many expectations, maybe my head was too filled with Disney princes to give a chance to real, living, breathing men. But here's the thing being with Nolan has taught me. And mind you, he's not perfect." A knowing chuckle. "Far from it. But what it has taught me is that if your guy wants to be with you, he'll be with you. He won't make excuses about his job or the timing or his ex who won't leave him alone. He won't be incapable of planning out a few dates." She's looking far away now, a sort of smile on her face. "That's the thing, I think, about us women. Sometimes, we either aim too high or too low. Either we have a list of twenty things down to the height, hair color, eye color, shoe size, and a bunch of shallow shit, or we just go for a guy who makes our heart jump a little, even if we've been with him half a dozen times and see how it ends. Wyn, from what you told me, a lot went on between you. Emerson said some pretty heavy things while you were at the resort. If he meant them, he'll be able to wait."

"But four months—"

Another snort. "Come on. People act like it's the hardest thing in the world. Do we not have porn now? I'm not saying it'll be easy for him. I'm just saying he'll do it." She shrugs. "I don't know, call me naive or out-of-touch because of Nolan. Maybe it's true. But what

I've found is when a guy really likes you, and I mean really, really likes you, all the other excuses that come into play with other men don't even figure. It won't matter if it's the right time or you're apart, or if he isn't technically, a hundred thousand percent in his heart, ready. It won't matter if you aren't his religion or even his usual type. It won't matter. Obstacles will just be a word he won't look twice at. If he's your guy, then Wynona, he'll walk through fire for you." She reaches out to give my shoulder a supportive squeeze. "And don't beat yourself up. I think that's what you did when you set him free a week ago. You wanted to see if he was worth his words. It's easy to be in love when you're alone with someone for two weeks on a tropical island. It's easy to be faithful and think everything will work when you don't have to work or live together or have to deal with any of the boring, troublesome BS that makes up actually building a life together. It's easy to be faithful when you see the person day in, day out. But can you do it for a few months away? I'm not saying to extend this longer than necessary. I'm not even saying that you shouldn't visit him. What I am saying is that it's been a week, and you didn't say 'not ever', you said 'not now', and for your guy, that would mean 'later'. Your guy would wait. And if he can't, if he can't handle being on his own and not getting his way, if he can't keep you in mind when you're not there, then what's the point?"

She exhales. "Sorry. I think I'm getting overly philosophical. It's Nolan's fault. He went on this"—air quotes— "spiritual journey. Anyway… I'm not going to get into it. My point is, Wyn, if he's not your guy, wouldn't you rather know now?"

I find myself nodding, my hands going to my stomach. "But my baby…"

"She's right," Josie says. "The best thing you can do for your baby is let its father make his own decisions. Yeah, it would be nice if things work out and you can all be a family. But just because he's the father of your child doesn't mean he's your guy. He has to earn the second part."

"You're right." I find that, somehow, I can smile and almost mean it. "Both of you." I wrap my arms around them again. "Thank you. I just... it's easy to forget, to let the old fears creep on in."

"Hey." Sierra tips her forehead against mine. She smells like the Shea butter we rubbed on our feet after we did that at-home pedicure earlier. "We've all been there. When you love someone so much, I don't know about you, but at the best times, it's crazy, but I find myself thinking there's no way this can work, can last. There's no way I can be this happy, that things can be this good and stay this way. That's the curse of the happiest times. You fear the fall."

"You wonder how they can like you, of all people," Josie says softly. "Out of all the people, they chose you. It seems crazy."

"Yeah," I say. Because they said it all already, and there's nothing left to say. "Yeah."

CHAPTER 24

Emerson

I walk alone to the bar so I can get my head around it.

I'm doing it. This is really my life.

Playing piano up on stage while the crowd goes wild, so into the music that I hardly notice.

The first big paycheck already came in, and while it went straight to my savings, it felt damn good.

Putting away money for the future.

For the first time in a while, I can see something there. It's still hazy, too hazy to put a real form to.

But it's there.

As I walk, I extend my arm experimentally. The midnight air is still spritzed with the rain that stopped less than an hour ago.

Maybe that was the best thing about tonight. How it was pouring out, too wet and miserable for anyone to bother with an outdoor concert. And yet, when we all strode out on the stage, there they were, crowding the field.

Young and old, men and women, smiling and scowling against the onslaught.

There for the music.

As I walk, I step into the reflection of my black sneakers over and over and over again.

Wynona always said it was the best time for artists, the way the puddling reflections cast and recast the light. She was the only one I knew who'd still jump into puddles for the splash.

Don't go there, Emerson.

So, I don't.

I keep on walking. I stretch my fingers in the stretch I use to keep the cramps away. I let the London moon stare at me amid the old-style buildings. I wonder how many are forgeries, how many the real thing.

I wonder that about people too. About myself.

I get to the bar before I realize it. One second, I'm scanning further down the street lined with old Greystone buildings, and the next there's a knock on the glass right beside my head.

I whirl around, and there they are. Inside the Willicker, the crew of the World Classical Tour in the flesh.

Kelvin Wyatt, the violinist, with his dreads, chocolate eyes, and a smile so bright it wakes me up a bit just looking at it. Howell looks like your favorite granny, only she's got hot pink hair, plays the sax like a demon, and has a voice like a chainsaw. Tarla smells like a different fruit every day—today it's lemon—and loves nothing more than a good arm wrestle. Oh, and she plays the viola like she was born with one.

And then there's Ky. Pretty, young, and she has a way of looking at you with those endless chocolate eyes that makes any sort of harmless half-truth seem naked. Her flute playing and singing come from deep down inside her, and they resonate deep down inside you, too.

"You did come," Kelvin says, giving me a whopping pat on the back.

"Of course he did," says Yolan, our leader. "Emerson's good to his word, I told you."

"Only he almost wasn't," Tarla points out, waggling a lemony freckled finger at me.

They all know how I almost didn't come on the tour at all.

I laugh good-naturedly. "I'm never going to catch a break for that, am I?"

"Nope," Tarla says just as good-naturedly.

"We were talking about love," Kelvin says with a wry smile as he sips his wine. "We've gone around the table and concluded that for most of us, our types are defined by our first love. Either we look for them endlessly or we seek out those most unlike them."

"Interesting," I say.

Ky looks at me like the only thing interesting is my response and what it means.

Tarla throws that bright head back and laughs and laughs. "I know a deflection when I hear it."

"I just don't have much to contribute," I say neutrally.

I suddenly want a glass in my hand, two or three beers down my throat.

I'm not drunk enough to deal with this. With her.

But she's there, all right, flashing in my head. I think we both know that's the solution. We separate for a time while you do this contract.

The sad finality in those blue eyes, like she knew that this could ruin everything, and still, still believed in the necessity of it.

Fuck.

"Here." Ky's handing me a drink with a small, intimate smile. "We ordered an extra."

I sip it and wait for the world to slacken. For her image—that dark glossy hair, those so changeable blue eyes, her pale skin—to recede out of my mind. For the tension to come out of my shoulders.

The others have ambled to the bar to get the next round. It's just me and Ky with her round moon face and her pale skin, her dark red hair and a smile I can never seem to get a handle on.

"You know what I think?" she says. "I think we never truly get over the disappointment of it. Not really. Not if it was real love. We settle and we find another—maybe even a better. But it lingers there like a slow cancer. Like when you find out Santa isn't real, or about global warming. You lose something primal. And I think a lot of us, we never get it back."

She sips her wine with a twisted sort of smile, and her eyes dance. "There's a sort of impossible magic to it. Like the world going from black and white to color all at once. Like you didn't realize life could be like this, this good."

She's not looking at me, of course. Her dark eyes are deeper than ever, and I know they're looking at him. Whoever he is. "I mean, two people with such different life experiences, at least to me, when I was a kid and then later, it seemed to me there'd be no way, no humanly possible way I'd find someone who got me, who I got. That they'd like me as much as I liked them, especially if they knew me. That was the one thing I was sure of—how could they like me if they knew me, when I didn't?"

Her smile's gone wistful. Her eyes still aren't on me. "And then you meet them, of course, and all of a sudden, the world opens. Like you'd only been squinting, so you'd never seen just how much possibility there is in this world. The nice old lady at the supermarket and the way the light dances on the water every night. The song of birds and the funny chipmunks stealing wrappers from each other. It's like fairy dust. Turns everything to gold.

"And when we lose it, all we want is to get it back. It doesn't matter how or why or if it's even right, if the magic's long-gone. We hunger for that first miracle, that first unfolding." Her eyes land on me. "Even if it's not right."

I drink the rest of my drink, thinking. I hardly noticed, but at some point, Ky stepped closer to me.

I understand now.

Who she reminds me of, and why.

It's her, of course it's her.

Wynona.

I came here to appease her, to spite her, to escape her, and here she is already.

It's easy to see how tonight will go … if I let it. How the drinks will ease the tightness of her absence. How she hasn't returned my texts or calls. How, maybe, they'll let another in, just to fill the space for a while.

I put my empty glass down on the table with the laughing others. "I have to go."

"Want company?" Ky says, already following me to the door.

"No," I say.

Although that isn't true.

I don't tell her, I want company, but not you.

I walk outside.

Just in time. The rain's decided a second, cooler act is in order.

God only knows what I think about that. I never did get my head around it, though.

How I can stand one week that already feels like four months. Without her.

CHAPTER 25

Wynona

The wisteria grows.

Purple pods propagate across the arm, joining freckles like a connect-the-dots that finally makes sense after all these years.

"Wisteria is poisonous," she said an hour or so ago, Jessica, when I asked her what made her choose it.

Roses, I've done so many I've lost count. A good number of sunflowers, lilies, jasmine, enough lotus and Buddhas to make me secretly itch to give the jolly fat guy a toupee or something totally wrong, like bunny ears, whenever I'm asked to tattoo another.

"Beautiful, but poisonous," Jessica said with a smile that didn't even reach her lips. One that I recognized all too well.

"It's to remember," she said.

"His name was Wyatt," she said.

And, as I add one purple poisonous pod after another to the bunch, it makes me wonder.

If one day I'll need my own tattooed reminder of what mistake to never make again.

If it even is.

It's been a month now. A month of questioning, of trying not to check on the tour's progress online, yet checking all the same.

When I go to take a break, Josie's sitting on the picnic bench behind my place, doodling with a big sun hat and a private smile. She snaps her book shut.

As she holds something out to me, I realize what yumminess I was smelling—chocolate croissants.

"Are you writing your pornos again?" I tease her, shaking my head.

Josie had this period, a few years back, when she'd never go anywhere without her fuzzy purple notebook. What she scrawled in it, she'd never say. Her 'pornos' was what we called it, alluding to who-knew-what. She never showed me.

Now, she's wearing a bright green dress covered with pink lollipops, eyeing me.

"What?" I say.

"Just... If I tell you something, do you promise not to get mad?"

"Nope," I say.

She sighs.

I sigh right on back, slinging myself down on the picnic bench. "How can I promise when I don't know what it is?"

"You and your logic," Josie says, taking a perturbed bite of her croissant, her bright red and yellow striped nails flashing in the noontime sun.

"All right, all right," she says a minute or so later, flipping open the notebook.

I glance and... stare.

"You did these?" I say.

"Yes, my pornos," Josie says with a giggle.

Only they aren't. They're people, men, women, kids, the odd dog—drawings of them. And they're good, really good.

"You draw," I say.

I'm not sure I'd be much more surprised if I saw Josie stealing a car. Drawing and Josie just don't go together. Like dogs and catnip. Or so I thought.

"I'm sorry," she says quietly. "I just... that was always your thing. I didn't want to take that away from you."

I smile at her a bit sadly. "I haven't always been the easiest person to be sisters with, have I?"

She's got her own sad one. "No. But it's okay."

And then we're hugging, and she's saying, "I didn't come here to tell you that."

I pull away, my glance saying it. Then what did you come here to tell me?

She swallows the last of the croissant. "I can tattoo, too."

I eye her. "Jesus. Who are you and what have you done with Josie?"

"All I wanted to say is that... the other night, a few weeks ago, it got me thinking. If you want to go after him, you can."

"Josie."

She holds up a finger. "Let me finish. I've been thinking about this a while. How you don't get too many second chances, if you get them at all. I've been tattooing on the side, here and there, for close to three years now. It's just a fun hobby. I'm not nearly as good as you, but I think I could pick up the business, at least for a while. Enough for you to go visit him, maybe even stay. A few weeks, a few months, half a year—"

"But Josie—"

"I've already talked to the nursery. They're okay with me taking a few months off if I need to. God knows, I've saved enough of their practically dead plants that they owe me."

When I don't say anything, she says, "Just think about it."

"What if…"

"Don't start like that." She's already shaking her head. "'What if' never got anyone anywhere useful, unless it was for science."

"Or history," I add.

She rolls her eyes. "Disregard everything I say, why don't you."

I turn to look at her.

It's weird. Sometimes, I see expressions on her face that I've seen in the mirror on myself.

"You really think I should go?" I ask quietly.

"What do you think?"

"I don't know."

Her smile isn't convinced. "Yes, you do."

"But, Jos—"

"There's no buts. You either make a go of it or you don't. What do you have to lose?"

"I made a decision."

"You can't make another one?"

Her words make a lot of sense. It doesn't help that they're saying the same thing as the thoughts in my head.

"It's just so sudden," I add.

Josie looks at me steadily. "Just admit it. You're afraid."

"And you wouldn't be?"

"I didn't say that."

And then we sit there in a silence that's another name for waiting. Finally, I get up. "I should head back in. Jessica's waiting. I can call you, though. Tonight?"

Josie's already off the picnic bench and two steps away. "All right. And Wyn?"

"Yeah?"

"Just make sure you don't go with fear and rename it logic."

Now I'm the one rolling my eyes. "Thanks, Socrates."

She winks. "Later, gator."

And I'm left to my thoughts and more wisteria.

It's a kind of meditation, tattooing. The canvas of the skin. The buzzing of the needle. My attention, like its own sort of hyper-focused needle.

Afterward, I head home. I make some lasagna. I successfully avoid thinking about it.

Until I am, and I know the only thing there is to do.

"You really are a pain, you know that?" is the first thing I say to Josie when she picks up the phone.

"Hello to you too," she says, and I can hear the smile in it. "So, you've come to your senses?"

"Meaning?"

She sighs. "When am I coming over?"

I grin. "Tonight too early?"

She grins too, I can just tell. "Hell no."

**

Twelve hours later, and I'm there. Who would've thought? In Paris, France. At the Philharmonie de Paris.

Watching Emerson Storm play the piano up on stage.

I'm surrounded by people with their friends and lovers. I'm by myself, but I don't feel alone.

I've never felt all that alone, not when there's music.

And here, oh, what music.

The kind of music to reach inside you and strum. Emerson plays piano like I didn't know it could be played.

My stomach growls for the candy apple stand I keep smelling, though I dare not go there. There's such a wall of a crowd between me and it.

Besides, I've got a man to watch. Music to listen to.

It's nighttime and cool enough that the breeze is pebbling my bare arms. I knew I should've brought that stupid hoodie.

But I wanted to look good for this. Not that he'll see me. What are the odds? I'm deep in the crowd, far from the front, and not tall. I keep having to shuffle from side to side to see around the big-headed fourteen-year-olds ahead of me.

I'm having the time of my life.

I'm scared. Terrified, actually. And yet, there's a relief in it.

I've made my choice, and maybe it will bury me, but at least I'll know.

Whether second chances are for real or for suckers. Whether Emerson's words were just that, words, or if they were staircases to somewhere real.

The crowd and I, we watch, listen. Emerson plays and plays and plays.

And then it's the end, and they're bowing.

And her, that girl, she leans in too close to him and says something, and he chuckles, pulling away, his gaze elsewhere. And then it stops.

On me.

He can't—

He can.

He does.

Emerson's looking at me. I can see his lips move—Is that—but can't hear what he's saying over the noise.

And then he strides to the microphone, grabs it. "Wynona?"

And he's looking straight at me.

The crowd is a sea of heads turning to look where he's looking.

"Wynona," he says into the microphone, his voice booming over the crowd. "Come up here."

The crowd is a sea of bodies stepping aside for me to walk through.

I almost laugh out of sheer terror and embarrassment and surprise.

This isn't real. This is the kind of thing that happens in books and movies to girls who are cooler and have better lives than me.

And yet, here I am.

I walk in the dream to him, this man who I'm not sure what he is anymore. All I know is that he's got a smile like it's Christmas and New Year's and Easter all at once.

And I've got it too.

I walk into his arms. He takes the microphone, and amid the cheers, he says, "This is my girlfriend. This, ladies and gentlemen, is the girl I'm going to marry someday."

And it's then, as the crowd goes wild and he gives me a kiss and pulls me offstage so it'll be just us, this moment, just ours, that I know.

No doubt, no holds barred, everything, absolutely everything, is going to be okay.

CHAPTER 26

Emerson

What a past few months.

Italy. Spain. Japan, Australia. Canada, and so many US cities I've lost track. A handful of islands.

The only constant thing has been her, Wynona.

My girlfriend. The mother of my child. And so much more.

Even when we miss our flight and have to nap on disheveled 60s-era airport benches, even when my wallet gets stolen, even when we have to sleep in the back of a beat-up rented camper van with my hoodie for a blanket, she makes it all bearable. Better than bearable, she makes it fucking amazing.

Sitting in the airport, she looks so pretty in that red skirt and black turtleneck that I can't help but kiss her.

"What was that for?" she asks with a giggle when we separate.

I shrug. "Nothing. Everything."

"Oh." She nods sagely. "That."

I put my arm around her and survey the scene. Nolan once said he went to airports to 'get material', since you see all types.

People at their laziest and worst. Sweats and shouts. Arguments and overpriced chip bags.

In Lebanon's airport, according to Greyson, they've got a glass pillar filled with confiscated weapons. Guns, knives, an axe or two.

"Emerson," Wynona says with a scolding tone.

It takes me a few minutes to catch on to why. My hand's slipped down to her belly.

One of my new habits lately. She claims it tickles.

"I can't help it," I say with a shrug. "What kind of father would I be if I ignored the little guy?"

Wynona just smiles, patting my hand a bit absently.

"Game time," I say.

She groans. "I told you—"

"We'll know when we see his little face, I know, I know." I shrug.

"Fine," she says. "Because I'm bored."

"Alastair," I say.

She quirks an eyebrow. "Is this baby going to be born old?"

"Have to be ready for all possibilities," I return stoutly.

She chuckles. "Fine. Joseph."

I look at her hard. "That's one of the most common names in the world. You really want him to be Joseph S. all his life?"

She shrugs. "I just really liked Joseph and the Amazing Technicolor Dreamcoat as a kid."

"Benjamin," I say.

She frowns. "For our firstborn? Come on. Robert."

"No."

"Why not?"

I shrug. "When I was a kid, the school douche everyone hated was named Rob."

She shrugs too. "Good enough for me. Not Robert, then."

"What were you talking to Ky about the other day?" I ask.

Out of all the surprises these past few months have brought me, that's been one of the biggest. Ky and Wynona are getting on famously.

"Oh, girl stuff, you know, engagements."

"Oh yeah? What about?"

"Just about the type of proposal itself," Wynona says musingly. "Whether we'd prefer one of those big in-public, maybe-even-a-YouTube-video kind, or something... less so."

"What was the verdict?" I ask like a man who hasn't planned to propose at our next concert.

"Private's best," Wynona says without a hint of hesitation.

I try to keep my face neutral.

"Public's too stressful," she explains. "And my reaction, it wouldn't feel like mine. It would feel like theirs, like I was doing it for them. I wouldn't trust my own smile."

She smiles a little. "That's just me, though. I've seen some that were really sweet, and I think it's great for most people. I'm just not most people, I guess."

"No." I take her hand in mine. "That you are not."

"So then," I continue, "hypothetically speaking, where would you be asked?"

"In a perfect world?" Her gaze wanders in thought. "I don't know, maybe... at home? Somewhere busy and loud, where no one would notice? Sometime when I'd least expect it."

Something clicks in my head.

I take a look around.

Busy?

—Check.

Loud?

—Check.

"All right." I get down on one knee.

"Emerson!" she exclaims.

"What?" I say.

"Don't joke like that," she leans down to hiss at me.

"Who's joking?"

"But, you can't here—"

"Why not?"

"People are staring. This isn't private."

"All right." I get up and pick her up. I hoist her bag onto my shoulder as well.

"Emerson!"

"What?"

"What are you doing?"

"Finding somewhere more private. Where people won't stare."

Her mouth is caught between a laugh and a grimace. "Seriously?"

"Seriously," I say. "Our flight's not for another two hours."

I carry her to the door. "Good thing we didn't go ahead and check in early."

"Were you planning this all along?" she demands.

"Nah. I had a much better plan. But apparently, it isn't your style."

"But now it won't be a surprise," she points out musingly.

"I can only surprise you so many times. You missed your chance."

She chuckles. "I suppose I deserve that."

"Besides," I say. "I could change my mind by the time we get there. You are arguing a lot."

"Jerk," she says.

"Nag," I say.

"Menace."

"Shrew."

She quirks an eyebrow. "Oh, we're going old-timey now? You yellow-bellied cur!"

I chuckle as I carry her out the airport doors. "You still remember that class? Shakespeare 101?"

She laughs. "I still remember your writing the answers to the final exam on that fat eraser."

I grin. "It got me to pass."

I pause, look around. One side of the building is crowded with taxis. The other isn't.

The other it is.

We walk along in silence as I carry her that way.

"Emerson?" she says quietly.

"Yeah?"

"When did you know?"

"Know what?"

"You know."

I pause. "Does it matter?"

"Emerson."

I shrug. "The minute I saw you in the crowd while on tour. I had thought about it before, but then, I knew."

"But we hadn't even traveled together or spent that much time…"

"It didn't matter. I just knew."

She moves against my chest, and I see tears sheening those beautiful blue eyes. "You're crazy."

I smile down at her. "You like it."

"Well, I'm crazy too, now aren't I?"

"Not going to argue with that."

And we laugh and laugh, and it occurs to me then that I've walked us around to a shady little garden where there's no one around. It isn't perfect—there's weeds and a pile of mud further on that might just be dog shit. Not exactly the dream spot for a proposal.

I could keep walking, keep looking for the perfect place. But here's the thing—the perfect place is where Wynona is.

And so, I put her down carefully.

"Emerson," she says.

I get down on one knee. "Wynona."

"God, are you actually…"

"Well, will you?"

She manages to clamp down her grin into a frown. "Will I what?"

"You know."

She glares at me. "Seriously?"

"All right," I growl. "Wynona Collins, will you marry me?"

She eyes me appraisingly, and I sigh.

"When I met you all those years ago," I continue, "I went home and made that song, our song. I pretended to make it up when you were there a few months later.

"Every girl I dated after you, I kept comparing, and they always came up short.

"You left a dirty sock at my place, this funny pink thing with smiley clouds on it. I've still got it, wedged in the back of some drawer.

"When I was drunk, my go-to used to be Googling you, sometimes going to your tattoo business page.

"I don't like how much I love you." I frown. "It's inconvenient. When we fight, it ruins my day. Do you ever wonder when it's almost too good to be true…"

"How it can last?" she asks quietly with a nod. "Yeah. Like it's so wonderfully, horribly good, it's bound to mess up. Somehow."

"But it hasn't," I say.

"It hasn't," she says, eyeing me with a look I can't place. "So, all that you said before, basically… you're a stalker?"

I chuckle. "Right, I forgot the shrine I have to you in my closet where I sacrifice baby spiders."

She giggles. "So."

I glare at her. "You going to make me say it again?"

"No."

"Then…"

"I'm just thinking."

"Of?"

She tips her head. "Whether I want to say 'yes, oh, God, yes!' or if that's a bit overdone."

"Why not just nod?"

She giggles. "Seriously?"

"Have you ever seen a movie couple do that? Or read a book where they do it?"

"It would be a first," she admits, her smile growing.

And then, blue eyes steady on me, slowly, she nods.

I rise, nodding too.

She nods back. "Weirdo."

I nod again. "Goof."

And then we kiss, still laughing.

Right now would be when they shoot the fireworks.

EPILOGUE

Wynona

"He really pulled it off," Sierra says, eyeing our gorgeous hilly surroundings with an approving smile.

We're sitting at a table on a hill, surrounded by a sweeping, green-grassed swath of other hills, beneath a deep blue sky. The air is the perfect compromise between hot and cool, fresh. It smells like life, with the slightest tinge of the sea.

"Scotland," Josie says with an awe in the name that isn't entirely undeserved, as the past few days we've spent here can attest. "Are you guys still going to check out Fingal's Cave?"

"If a weirdly geometric cave is good enough for Pink Floyd, it's good enough for us," I say. "But first, the honeymoon."

Josie snorts. "Hasn't your whole relationship been a honeymoon?"

"Kind of," I admit.

"And he still won't tell you what it is?" Josie presses.

I shrug. "Nope. After I told him I don't want any more trips, he said he'd have to think it over."

"Isn't that the definition of a honeymoon, though, a trip?" Sierra asks, twirling a brown-red strand around her finger.

"Wait, I've got this," Josie says, taking out her phone. "According to Oxford Languages, a honeymoon is a vacation spent together by a newly married couple."

"And vacation?" Sierra asks.

"An extended period of leisure and recreation, especially one spent away from home or in traveling," Josie says.

"Well, that leaves options," I say with a chuckle. "I guess?"

Josie just laughs. "Typical Wynona. Ask for something impossible."

My gaze strays to Emerson, where he's chatting with his brothers and Jeremy, glancing at me. We share a smile. "And I got it."

"That you did," Josie says, leaning in. "So, tell me, what is happily ever after like?"

I roll my eyes. "Oh, you know, it's just glorious."

"No, really," she says. "Single lady asking here."

"I… it's hard to explain," I admit.

"Try me."

"It's good. I'm really happy," I say.

Josie's golden lashes flicker as she shifts in her satin blue bridesmaid's dress. "Why do I feel like there's a 'but' in there?"

I shrug a little with a laugh. "You always find new things to want, to hope for."

Sierra nods. "The ol' human condition bit."

I grin. "But being with Emerson has already taught me a lot. It's made me realize how I want things to be for our son. How I want to be for our son."

"Which is?"

I gesture around at our surroundings. Our family and friends are gathered here, all in celebration. The wafts of delicious food, roasted meat of every type, every side dish you could think of, and enough pastries to gorge yourself and die happy.

"This," I say. "Happy. Or as happy as I can be."

Josie snorts. "So, basically, you're going to become me?"

I chuckle. "Up on yourself, much?"

She blows me a kiss.

"Seriously, though," I say, more quietly now. "How do you do it?"

"Do what?" Josie asks.

"When something shitty happens, I've seen you get upset, but… it doesn't ever seem to stick. How?"

Josie takes a few seconds to think about it.

"I don't know," she finally admits. "I just… for me, it's always been more practical. Maybe I'm just really good at lying to myself and seeing only what I want to see, but it's always turned out better that way. It's just a choice. A habit. A repetition."

I nod. "I can do that. Maybe. I can try, at least."

Just then, Emerson approaches the table, his eyes on me.

"All right, all right," Sierra says to him with a sigh. "We'll let you have your wife back."

A smile pulls up the side of his mouth. "Thanks."

"First dance?" I say as I rise.

"First dance," he says.

And suddenly, the band is playing a Whitney Houston song.

Emerson takes me to the dance floor, puts his arms around me, and we move together.

I give a little happy twinge under the intensity of his gaze. "Stop it."

"Stop what?" he asks.

"How you're looking at me. I'm going to trip over my own two feet."

His response is instantaneous, sure. "Then I'll catch you."

"Jerk."

"Wife."

I chuckle. "Ugh, just say it, then."

"Say what?"

"Emerson."

Still, we're dancing, moving, though I've lost track of everything else other than him.

"Can't we just enjoy this dance?"

My smile is merciless. "Nope."

He tries to frown and fails. "Fine."

"I'm going to release some songs, I think," he says. "Dedicate them to you and our son."

"That's amazing, but…"

"Why now?" His gaze goes faraway. "It sounds stupid but… forget it."

"No," I hiss. "You are not holding out on me on our freaking wedding day, Emerson Storm."

"All right." A smile touches the corners of his lips. "You're my miracle, Wynona Storm. After you, I stopped believing in second chances or that life was anything other than a toss of random happenstance, good or bad, that we had little choice over."

"And now?" I say softly.

"Now, I don't know what I believe. Except that second chances are possible, way more than I ever thought. And it's because of you."

He kisses my next words out of my mouth, and the crowd goes wild. Somewhere along the way, the song changes, and the patch of grass where we're dancing is filled with other happily dancing couples.

The rest of the night is a dream. We dance and eat and drink lemonade until the moon comes out to watch. And then, without warning, Emerson pulls me away.

"I've one more surprise for you."

"What is it?" I ask.

"It's our honeymoon."

I get tired running up the hill, so he carries me. At the crest, he holds me, and we look down. On the horizon, in the moonlight, I can see...

"Is that..." I begin.

"It is," he says. "It's our future. Our honeymoon."

"Hold on." I spin to study him, his face, for signs that he's joking. But I don't find any. "But that's..."

"A castle," he says. "Yeah. My brothers and I bought it together. Right now, you and I have it to ourselves for as long as we want."

Even from far away, I can see that it's massive, gorgeous, surrounded by sprawling empty hills.

"Come on," he says, and he takes me there. "It's ours. All of it."

Inside, it's even more beautiful. Ceilings so high your voice echoes, gorgeous antique furniture. And in our room, in our four-poster bed, we make love for the first time in our castle home.

As we come in each other's arms, I understand.

This is what happily-ever-after feels like.

~The End~

If you LOVED His Second Chance, be sure to check out other books by Ashlee Price!

Surprise Bidder

Kitchen Boss

Most Eligible Daddy

Best Friends Ex with Benefits

Check them out here on my webpage

https://www.ashleepriceromanceauthor.com/

Amazon lists millions of titles, and I'm happy you discovered this one.

But if you'd like to know when I release a new book, instead of leaving it up to chance, sign up for my newsletter.

I'll send you an email when my latest release goes live.

https://www.ashleepriceromanceauthor.com/signup/